THE SOCIETY OF SUPER SECRET HEROES

The Great Cape Rescue

THE SOCIETY OF SUPER SECRET HEROES

The Great Cape Rescue

by PHYLLIS SHALANT

Dutton Children's Books

Dutton Children's Books

A division of Penguin Young Readers Group

PUBLISHED BY THE PENGUIN GROUP / Penguin Group (USA) Inc., 375 Hudson Street, New York, New York 10014, U.S.A. / Penguin Group (Canada), 90 Eglinton Avenue East, Suite 700, Toronto, Ontario, Canada M4P 2Y3 (a division of Pearson Penguin Canada Inc.) / Penguin Books Ltd, 80 Strand, London WC2R 0RL, England / Penguin Ireland, 25 St Stephen's Green, Dublin 2, Ireland (a division of Penguin Books Ltd) / Penguin Group (Australia), 250 Camberwell Road, Camberwell, Victoria 3124, Australia (a division of Pearson Australia Group Pty Ltd) / Penguin Books India Pvt Ltd, 11 Community Centre, Panchsheel Park, New Delhi - 110 017, India / Penguin Group (NZ), 67 Apollo Drive, Mairangi Bay, Auckland 1311, New Zealand (a division of Pearson New Zealand Ltd) / Penguin Books (South Africa) (Pty) Ltd, 24 Sturdee Avenue, Rosebank, Johannesburg 2196, South Africa / Penguin Books Ltd, Registered Offices: 80 Strand, London WC2R 0RL, England

CIP Data is available.

Published in the United States by Dutton Children's Books,
a division of Penguin Young Readers Group,
345 Hudson Street, New York, New York 10014
www.penguin.com/youngreaders

Designed by Heather Wood

Printed in USA / First Edition

ISBN 978-0-525-47404-3
1 3 5 7 9 10 8 6 4 2

TO HERB,
MY SUPERHERO

CONTENTS

THE SOCIETY OF SUPER SECRET HEROES

The Great Cape Rescue

LABOR DAY

It was a holiday for most people, but not all. The workers at the fast-food restaurants were still serving burgers and fries. Lifeguards were still guarding swimmers at the town pool. Many busy moms and dads were catching up on household chores. And superheroes were doing their best to save people before the first day of school tomorrow.

"Hurry, the Horrible Hypnotizer is getting away!" Finch shouted as he rounded the corner of the house. "Keep your eyes closed in case he turns around. If he puts the chicken trance on you, you could be laying eggs for the rest of your life."

The guys were right behind Finch, running with their eyes shut, too. It was a good thing they knew the yard so well. Rajiv felt the azalea hedge scratch at his T-shirt. Kevin's fingertips brushed the drainpipe that ran down the side of the house. Elliott was laughing so hard, he tripped over the apple-tree root that was shaped like an alligator—and bumped into Finch.

Smack! Thud! Pop! Crash!

Finch opened his eyes. His sister, Mimi, was sprawled on the front walk.

"You pinheads! Why don't you look where you're going?" she shouted. The contents of her pool bag—towel, wet bathing suit, magazine, hairbrush, suntan lotion, and lip gloss—were scattered everywhere. She swept her long brown hair out of her face and smirked at the boys. "I bet you were playing stupid-heroes again."

Finch reached over and handed her the pink flip-flop that had flown off her foot. "Sorry. But we weren't playing. We were practicing saving the world."

"Get real, will you?" Mimi stood up and brushed off the back of her shorts. "You'd better not play that baby game when you start fourth grade tomorrow—

unless you want to be known as the class losers all year."

Mimi (as in "Me! Me!" Finch thought) was going into seventh this year. She acted like she knew everything. It really drove Finch crazy, especially when she was right.

With one hand on her hip, Mimi watched the boys collect her things. She didn't help. She just stood there in one of her many supermodel poses. This time it was the round-shouldered, droopy-eyelids one that made Finch think of a grouchy lizard.

Elliott stooped down to retrieve her suntan lotion from under the hedge. "Ooh, I feel dizzy," he said as he stood up. "I guess it's the sun or something." He pressed a palm to his forehead and closed his eyes.

"It's probably from eating junk food all day," Mimi sneered. This summer she'd only been willing to eat yogurt, salads, and tofu.

"Who are you, the Food Police?" Elliott groaned. His hair fell in his eyes as he bent forward and hugged his middle. Before Mimi could answer him, he began to gag. Everyone stepped back.

"Ack . . . ack . . . ack . . . blechhh!" Elliott was convulsing like a human volcano. A splat of yellow vomit flew through the air. It landed on Mimi's bare foot.

"Yeee-uck!" Mimi squealed. She flapped her foot. The vomit flew off and skipped twice on the front path before it settled down.

"Don't worry, I'll clean it up." With his bare hand, Elliott snatched up the mess and tossed it on his palm. The vomit bounced lightly.

Mimi's nostrils flared in a very unmodelish way. "That's rubber vomit!"

"Doh, no—it's *super*-vomit." Elliott slipped the fake vomit back into the big, deep pocket of his cargo shorts.

As the guys cracked up, Mimi grabbed her bag and swung it at them. It caught Finch right in the chest.

"Oww! Hey, that hurt!"

"A real superhero wouldn't complain about a little pain," Mimi said as she flounced toward the house. "Good luck in school, super-babies. You're going to need it."

"Yech, she said the S word," Finch grumbled when she was gone.

"Don't worry." Raj clapped a hand on his shoulder. Behind his wire-rimmed glasses, he winked an eye. "She'll probably have a fit tomorrow morning when she can't find this." He flashed his empty palm to the group. Then he closed it into a fist. When he opened it again, Mimi's lip gloss was there. "Ta-da! Raj the Remarkable strikes again," he crowed.

"Cool," Kevin and Elliott both exclaimed.

"Yeah, great trick," Finch said. Usually he admired Raj's skills as a magician, but right now his heart wasn't in it. At the beginning of summer, when he'd learned that Rajiv Shah, Kevin Chan, and Elliott Levenson—his three best friends—would be in his class, he'd been really psyched. Last year, none of them had been in Mrs. Rooney's room with him. But now that the time was here, Finch wasn't feeling so enthusiastic about going back to school. Mimi had told him that the fourth-grade teachers were as mean as trolls. They gave tons of work. They didn't even let the students have snack time.

"Where'd you get the vomit?" Kev asked Elliott.

"I found it on a Web site called Gag-o-Rama that sells funny stuff. It's supposed to be pizza vomit. Did you see the bits of pepperoni in it?"

"Yeah, gross. The person who made it is a real artist." Kev was an artist himself. So were both his parents. "Let's get to work on the comic. We should finish it today, because tomorrow"—he drew a

finger across his throat—"we'll probably have the H word—homework."

"All right." Finch opened the front door. It felt like it weighed a ton.

"Super Ferrets!" Rajiv cried as Cubby and Rosie came scampering at them across the hall floor. The two furry ferrets, one as pale as cream and the other the color of cinnamon, tumbled at the boys' feet. Rajiv picked Cubby up and draped him around his neck. Elliott wore Rosie.

They piled into Finch's room and sat down on the floor to play with the ferrets. But first they had to shove Finch's pajama bottoms, an empty chip bag, a sticky glass, towels, dirty socks, comics, a Batmobile, and other stuff into the corners. While Finch searched his desk, his buddies slid Cubby and Rosie across the floor like hockey pucks. It was the ferrets' favorite thing to play. But as the game got wilder, they crashed into each other. Rosie went skittering off into Finch's closet.

"Come back here!" Elliott crawled into the dark, crammed space and poked under the junk that was jumbled on the floor. Suddenly there was a scrabbling noise. Rosie ran out.

"Fin?" Elliott's voice sounded muffled. "You know that report on dolphins you lost last year? I think I found it. Hey, I didn't know you still had this!"

Finch quit hunting around in his desk and looked up. El was crawling out of the closet with his old superhero cape—a jewel-green beach towel decorated with yellow lightning bolts and green satin strings that tied around the neck.

Stop dragging me—I am not a floor mop!

For a moment Finch imagined he'd heard the cape complaining. Ugg. The day-before-school jitters were really driving him crazy.

He snatched the cape out of Elliott's hand and flung it back into the closet. "I don't wear that thing anymore. I didn't even know it was in there. Besides, you still have Ruff on your bed." Ruff was the stuffed dog Elliott had gotten as a baby. His mother had brought it along with her on the day she'd adopted him.

Elliott's eyes bugged out. "So?"

"So I still have Urp on mine," Raj said, reminding them of the cheerful sock monkey his grandmother had made for him. "And Kev has Blue Bunny. Calm down. Let's get back to the comic."

Finch extracted the latest edition of their series, *Super Ferrets,* from the mess on his desk. This one—*Super Ferrets' Swim Olympics*—was the first they'd done since last spring. The guys wrote the stories together, but Kev drew all the pictures.

"We're up to the part where Rosie climbs the shower curtain to get ready for her dive." Kev reached for a black marker.

Elliott peered over Kev's shoulder. "That reminds me of a new joke I made up. Who is the wizard who lives in the bathroom?"

Kev shrugged. "I give up."

"Harry Potty!"

All four guys cracked up. The ferrets loved it. They got up on their hind legs and began doing the weasel war dance, bobbing their heads and crying *dook, dook, dook, dook*. Then they jumped on each other.

"Wait, I've got another one," Elliott said before they'd stopped laughing. "What is the name of Harry Potty's school?"

"What?" Raj asked.

"Buttwarts!"

This time, the boys dooked like Rosie and Cubby.

"Shh, I think I just heard someone knock," Kev said.

"Finch? Boys?"

Finch's mom, Elaine Mundy, opened the door. She was tall and slim with long, straight brown hair like Mimi. Fin was more skinny than slim. He mostly looked like his dad. They both had dark, curly hair and ears that stuck out. Mr. Mundy could actually wiggle his.

"I'm going to fire up the grill for a barbecue," Mrs.

Mundy said. "Who wants hamburgers? Who wants tofu burgers?"

"Are the tofu burgers for Mimi?" Elliott asked innocently as he pushed his long hair out of his eyes. "'Cause I think I heard her say she wanted pepperoni pizza."

FIN'S SECRET

After the barbecue, the guys climbed up to the lookout platform Fin and his father had built in the biggest tree in the yard. They lay on their backs and watched as the sun sank lower in the sky.

Raj checked his watch. "This is the last hour of our last day of freedom together," he said in a voice of doom. "And the last day of being superheroes. Tomorrow we'll just be students."

"We can still be superheroes at lunch. We don't have to listen to Mimi," Elliott protested.

Kev sat up. "Forget it. No one at school is going to catch me pretending anymore."

"Kev's right," Raj agreed. "I don't want to be the class joke."

The guys were silent for a while. Then Finch said, "What if we weren't pretending?" His words seemed to hang in the air like the last note of a bird's song.

Raj rolled onto his side to face him. "What do you mean?"

"Superheroes help people who need it and keep bad stuff from happening. They fight for truth and justice. We could try to do that together. We could be like the X-Men or the Fantastic Four."

"Yeah, but superheroes have superpowers," Kev pointed out. "Where are we going to get ours—the mall?"

Elliott giggled. "Yeah, maybe there's a shop called Powers 'R' Us."

Finch felt the tips of his ears turning red. "I guess it's a dumb idea."

Raj sighed. "Not dumb, just impossible. I guess we'll have to be ourselves."

"I don't think that's so bad," El said.

That night, Finch tossed and turned until he was wrapped up in his sheets like a mummy. What if Mimi was telling the truth? What if all you did in fourth grade was work, work, work? He didn't think he was ready for so much maturity. Last year, Mrs. Rooney had given the class a little free time on Fridays. If Fin's desk wasn't overflowing with junk, she let him use the school photocopier to run off *Super Ferrets* for kids who wanted to read it.

Suddenly he felt it again—the pulling sensation. It was as if a giant magnet were in his closet, drawing him to it. "No!" he murmured as he grabbed the sides of the mattress.

I am here, Master.

Now it was talking. This was ridiculous. Finch put a pillow over his head. But his legs were practically sliding off the bed on their own. For a moment he listened to make sure no one was up. Then he reached into his closet and snatched the cape up off the floor.

When he was five, he'd found it at a garage sale his mother had insisted on stopping at on their way to her lawyer's office. It was the year his parents got separated. They'd told him it would just be for a bit. Finch had worn the cape to kindergarten every day while he waited for his father to move back in. That never happened, but at least he'd met the guys. They'd played superheroes on the playground each afternoon. A lot of other kids joined in too, but at the end of the term, Finch, Raj, Kev, and El were one another's best friends.

What he'd said today about not wearing the cape anymore wasn't exactly true. He'd stopped wearing it in first grade when some older kids started calling him Towelman. Instead he'd started sleeping with it like an extra blanket. Finally, when it didn't cover his feet anymore, he'd stowed it in the closet. But sometimes, after the lights were off, he still took it out. He knew he was too old for it—and he was going to stop. He just needed it one more night.

He folded the cape into a square and set it on top of his pillow. When he laid his head down, he imagined he felt a cool breeze against his cheek.

Sleep well, Master.

WELCOME TO FOURTH GRADE

Five lines were written on the chalkboard when the students arrived.

> *Mr. Slope Burns*
> *Birthplace: Felton, California*
> *Likes: Yoga, Music, Animals,*
> *Cold-Weather Sports*
> *Dislikes: Wearing a tie*

Mr. Burns didn't look old enough to be a teacher. He had unruly, orangey-red hair and wide cheeks with freckles. He was so skinny, his head nodded on his neck like a bobblehead doll. “Sit anywhere you want,” he said as the students looked around the room. He’d already set up the desks in little clusters of twos, threes, and fours.

Right away kids began dashing around, climbing over desks and other kids to be near their friends. *Bam!* Pierre tossed a chair to Alex, but Alex didn’t catch it. Tyler and Mike were having a tug-of-war with a desk, although there were plenty of empty ones still around. Someone tripped Kayla Keyes, who got a bloody nose and had to go to the nurse’s office.

Finch, Raj, Kev, and Elliott dove for a group of four desks near the back wall. It was a great spot—far enough away from the teacher so they could whisper jokes and stuff. Then two boys crash-landed into the set of desks on their left.

“Ugg,” Finch groaned. He turned away, but not quickly enough.

“What are you looking at, ferret face?” one of the boys asked. He had blond, spiky hair and eyes that looked like slivers of gray ice.

“Heh-heh, heh-heh,” the other boy snickered. Everyone called him Bud, but his real name was Norman Rosebud. Fin and his friends thought that was hilarious. For a rosebud, the guy was a real stinker.

Suddenly a strange sound blared out above the voices and the scuffling. It sounded like this: *Flaaah!* It was so loud it made several kids jump. Everyone stared at Mr. Burns. He was holding a bugle.

"Awesome," the teacher said. "You've already learned that when I blow this bugle, it means be quiet."

There was a burst of giggling and murmuring.

Flaaah! Flaaah! Flaaaaaaaaaaaaah!

Instantly, the room was as silent as if it were empty.

"Good. Now let's try this again. Quickly and quietly, find a desk." Mr. Burns chose to sit on top of his desk. He folded his legs in the lotus position, which Finch recognized from his mother's yoga videotape. The teacher's hands were resting on his knees, and his eyes were closed.

The students shot one another looks, but no one dared to laugh as they chose their places.

"That's much better," Mr. Burns said when he'd opened his eyes. "I'll pass around a seating chart now. When it gets to you, print your name beneath the desk you've selected. You can take a look at the learning centers I've set up while you're waiting."

Finch peered around at the Science Lab, the Banking Center, the Art Studio, and the Just for Fun table. But his eyes stopped when he spotted the Critter Corner. He loved animals—any kind. He'd always wanted a dog, but his mom was allergic, so they'd gotten ferrets instead.

"Now that you're in fourth grade, you're probably ready for more freedom and responsibility," Mr. Burns said when he had the seating chart back.

Oh boy, here it comes, Fin thought.

"During lesson time, we'll all work together. But during free time, you may go to any center you choose. There will be extra-credit activity sheets in each area. I think you'll find they're fun to do—and they're a great way to boost your grades."

Finch sat up straighter. So far, things didn't sound too bad.

"You'll also have jobs," Mr. Burns continued. "For

example, some of you will be responsible for keeping each learning center neat, and even adding little improvements."

Keeping things neat? Ugg. Finch slumped in his chair. That sounded like one of his mother's ideas. Personally, he didn't enjoy being neat or organized.

Mr. Burns slapped his palms against his knees. "All right, any questions?"

One arm waved. It belonged to the boy who had called Finch "ferret face."

No, Mr. Burns, no! Fin tried signaling his teacher with brain waves. *Don't call on him! Pretend you don't notice him!*

Mr. Burns was not a mind reader. He consulted the seating plan. "Irwin, right?"

The students shifted in their seats. No one called Irwin Thornton by his real name. Not even his teachers.

"Everyone calls me Thorn," he said.

"All right, Thorn."

"I was wondering if this was your first time teaching?"

"It is."

Thorn nodded smartly, as if he knew he'd been right. "Well, I was thinking you could use someone to be your personal assistant. A person who would collect the homework, make sure everyone was back on time from recess, and who could help you keep order around here. 'Cause I'd be good at that." Thorn crossed his arms over his chest.

"You mean like a policeman?" Chloe exclaimed.

"I'd rather say 'law enforcement officer,'" Thorn answered. "But don't call out."

Finch covered his eyes with his hand. Letting Thorn keep order would be like hiring a burglar to run the bank. The wannabe officer had just moved to Middleburgh last year. He'd been in Fin's class then, too. For a while Fin had thought he was funny. Sometimes they'd traded jokes or shared snacks.

But at lunch recess, Finch always hung out with Raj, Kev, and Elliott. In the past they'd played superheroes, although once they thought up *Super Ferrets*, they mostly worked on the comic. But Thorn kept stealing their paper and making it into airplanes, or using their pencils for "dart practice." When Finch complained to his teacher, she suggested that he and the guys invite Thorn to help them. "He's new here, Fin. Perhaps he just needs some friends," she'd explained.

So they'd tried it. But Thorn was bossy. The only

ideas he liked were his own. He wanted the ferrets to get run over by garbage trucks and grilled on barbecues.

"The comic is supposed to be about super ferrets, not dead ferrets," Finch told him.

"You said you wanted it to be funny. Barbecued ferrets are funny," Thorn had retorted. He'd gotten up and walked away, making sure to step on their drawings. It was the last time the guys worked on *Super Ferrets* in school. Or asked Thorn to join them for anything.

"I don't think this class is going to require an enforcer," Mr. Burns said, waking Finch from the aggravating memory.

Thorn shrugged. "O-kaaay, but I think you're making a mistake."

With a thumb, Mr. Burns stroked his bugle. He closed his eyes as if he were reconsidering.

Finch held his breath.

"I don't think so," Mr. Burns said finally. "I think I've made the correct decision."

"Yes!" Finch whispered louder than he'd meant to. Then he snuck a peek at Thorn. Unfortunately, Thorn was looking at him, too.

THE GIFT OR THE CURSE

"Now I'd like you all to write a composition about the best day you had this summer," Mr. Burns said.

The class moaned and groaned—except for a few writer kids, who immediately began lining up their pencils like soldiers. Sadly, Finch wasn't one of them.

"Come on. Everyone must have had at least one good day they can share. It will help me get to know you better." Mr. Burns's smile began to flatten out. It made Finch want to help him.

The scuffing sound of pencils on paper filled the

room. Finch's hand held a pencil, but it was frozen in midair. His summer included two best days, and he hated having to decide between them. One was when his mom took him and the guys to see the new *Spider-Man* movie. They'd had a sleepover afterward and stayed up really late talking about whether they'd want to have "the gift or the curse." It would be cool to swing around the neighborhood on super-spider threads, but as Peter Parker (who was actually Spider-Man) had put it, "With great power comes great responsibility." If you were a superhero, you'd be busy all the time saving people from bad guys, fires, earthquakes, and other stuff. There might not be much room for fun.

Finch's other "best day" was when he and his dad built the lookout platform in the yard. He'd wanted an entire tree house, but his father had said it would take too much time. Since he'd had a new baby with his new wife, Finch's dad was always in a rush. Still, Finch had to admit he'd liked working alongside his father. And the platform had turned out really awesome. You could see all over the neighborhood without anyone knowing you were up there.

All by itself, Finch's hand with the pencil moved

down to his paper. It began writing about building the lookout. Probably everyone had seen *Spider-Man*, anyway.

"Okay, who wants to read first?" Mr. Burns asked when it appeared that everyone was done working.

No one volunteered.

Mr. Burns squinted at the class. He looked down at his worn black high-tops. He sighed. He looked up again.

Elliott raised his hand.

"Elliott—you're on!" Mr. Burns exclaimed.

Elliott bopped up to the front of the room. Ever since Finch had known him, he'd been telling jokes, imitating the voices of their favorite cartoon characters, and acting out TV shows.

"This summer I went to a performing-arts camp at the college where my mom teaches. We did our own *American Idol* show. A lot of us were contestants, and a few campers got to be judges. All the girls tried to sing like pop stars. The guys did rap or hip-hop. But I sang 'Hakuna Matata' from *The Lion King,* and I was picked to be one of the finalists. At the end of camp, our friends and family were invited to see the last show. Fin, Raj, and Kev came. I got first prize." As if he'd just performed his song again, Elliott gave a little bow. His amber hair dropped over his eyes like the final curtain.

"Awesome," Mr. Burns said. "Does anyone have a question or a comment for Elliott?"

The class's three brainiac girls—Chloe, Zoe, and Kayla—waved in unison. Thorn's arm sprang up at the same time.

"What did you wear?" Chloe asked.

"A meerkat costume. I had ears, a tail, and a black nose."

The class cracked up at the thought of Elliott as a meerkat.

"What did you win?" Zoe asked.

"A one hundred percent fake gold trophy."

"Do you want to be a singer when you grow up?" Kayla asked.

"Yep—or an actor." Elliott began heading back to his desk.

"You forgot to call on Thorn," Bud pointed out.

"Raise your hand if you have something to say," Mr. Burns told him.

Bud's hand popped up. "He forgot—"

"Okay, okay," Elliott said. "Thorn."

Thorn leaned back in his chair. He grinned in a friendly way. "You know, you couldn't be a real singer or actor."

Finch felt his stomach tighten. If he were the teacher, he'd throw Thorn out before he said another word. But Mr. Burns was just sitting there.

Elliott's gaze was calm and steady. "Why not?"

Thorn spoke each word slowly and clearly. "Because—you—talk—funny."

Fin squirmed as if he were the one being picked on. It was true that Elliott rushed his words. And that he had trouble pronouncing his *l*'s, which he sort of gargled. But he'd been going to speech therapy since first grade. It was hardly noticeable anymore.

"Correction. I don't just talk funny—I *am* funny," Elliott said snappily.

Chloe's arm shot up. "Mr. Burns, that wasn't really a question or a comment. It was an insult."

"You're right, Chloe," Mr. Burns agreed. He pinned Thorn with a hard look. "Irwin, you owe Elliott and the rest of the class an apology."

"Sorrreee. Can I be next to read?"

Mr. Burns looked around as if he were hoping for

a different volunteer. But no one else wanted to be grilled by the team of Thorn and Bud. "All right," he said finally.

Thorn strolled up to the front of the room. He flapped a crease out of his paper and cleared his throat. "On the night of my birthday—JULY FOURTEENTH—I watched three *Star Wars* movies. It took six hours. I started at midnight and finished at six a.m. While I was watching, I ate six grape Popsicles. Afterward, my teeth were purple for two weeks. It was a great birthday." Thorn grinned. His teeth were only a disappointing yellow. "Any questions?"

One hand shot up—Bud's. "Who is your favorite *Star Wars* character and why?"

"Darth Vader—'cause he's the only superhero who's not wimpy."

"Darth Vader is not a superhero," Finch objected—but only inside his head.

Chloe raised her hand.

"Ask something rude," Fin muttered. He wished he had the nerve to do it himself.

"Yeah, ask if he's really an alien," Kev agreed, without looking up from the paper he was doodling on.

"Was your mom mad that you ate a whole box of Popsicles?" Chloe asked.

"Nope. She always lets me eat whatever I want. Sometimes I have cake or pie for dinner."

"Ew. I hope your dad is a dentist."

"Nope, he owns the Drop 'n' Shop." Thorn bounced on his toes. "It's open twenty-four hours a day. You can get Popsicles anytime you want there. You should stop in sometime. A Popsicle might take that sour look off your face."

"Sit down, Irwin," Mr. Burns ordered.

Kev slid the drawing he'd been making to Raj. Raj pressed his lips together to keep from laughing. He passed the paper to Finch next.

Finch looked down. Kev had drawn a character with spiky hair sprouting like grass from the top of his helmet. Two sharp fangs stuck out from the mask covering his face. Underneath Kev had printed THORN VADER.

Fin snorted. He shoved the paper toward Elliott. It flew off El's desk and onto the floor—just as Thorn was passing by. Thorn scooped it up and glanced over it. His face turned the color of a grape Popsicle. Then he balled it up in his fist.

Strangely, Finch felt as though he were watching his head being crushed.

SODAMAN AND SPRAYBUDDY

Finch reached into his backpack to grab his lunch. But as he felt around for his sandwich bag, his fingers touched something else. He'd know that feeling anywhere—soft, nubby cloth and smooth, satin strings. It was his cape! He gritted his teeth so hard a muscle in his jaw throbbed. His stupid sister! She was probably hoping he'd pull it out in front of all his classmates. He bet she was still laughing about it right now. Well, she wouldn't think it was funny tomorrow when she found her backpack stuffed with his dirty socks.

"Hurry up, Fin. What's taking you so long?" Raj asked behind him. "You're wasting precious time. El and Kev went to the cafeteria to save a table."

"Coming," Finch muttered. He pushed the cape to the bottom of his backpack and pulled out the brown paper bag that held his sandwich.

Perchance you should take your beverage, too, Master.

Fin's stomach fluttered. There was that voice in his head again. But it was right—he'd forgotten his juice box. He reached in and grabbed it. Once more he began buckling the flap.

Have a pleasant repast.

Fin hadn't realized he'd known the word *repast*, yet he was sure it meant something like "meal." Fourth-grade brains really *are* more mature, he thought.

"C'mon, I'll beat you to the repast room," he told Raj. Then he started to run, even though it was against the rules.

"I think I just saw the Horrible Hypnotizer behind those trees along the fence," Elliott whispered when they were out in the school yard after lunch.

Fin glanced around. "We can't play superheroes at school. If someone notices, we're dead."

"Don't tell me you're going to listen to your sister," Elliott said. "Besides, no one's watching. The Hypnotizer is putting a spell on all the kids—they're starting to act as dumb as chickens. We've got to stop him!"

Raj shook his head. "Man, you're crazy. If we start running around like we're superheroes, we're the ones who are going to look as dumb as chickens."

But their feet were already leading them toward the trees along the fence. It was as if they were under the Hypnotizer's trance.

"We're just taking a walk around the yard," Finch said firmly. "That's all."

"Right. Walking is good exercise," Raj agreed, striding easily on his long legs. "My parents do it every morning before work."

"Walking is boring," Kev grumbled. He was the shortest of the four guys, so he had to work harder to keep up.

"Shh! I think the HH is behind the last tree in the corner," Elliott whispered.

They broke into a trot. At first Finch squinted. Then he let his lids close. He loved moving with his eyes shut—it made him feel as if he'd stepped off the earth. He kept his arms out slightly so he wouldn't run into anything.

"I got him, I got him!" Elliott cried out. "I've got the Hypnotizer! Quick, help me blindfold him!"

"I got him, I got him!" a flat voice echoed. "Goody-goody."

"Take that, Hypnotizer!" someone else squealed in a high, silly tone.

Finch's stomach rocked. Even before he opened his eyes, he knew whose voices those were.

"The Hypnotizer? That's a good one. Maybe you could catch the Tooth Fairy next," Thorn jeered.

Bud snorted with laughter. He stood on his toes and whispered something in Thorn's ear.

Thorn's icy eyes fixed on Finch. "Did you say Finny isn't really Finny?" he asked loudly. "He's actually that famous superhero Towelman?"

Finch winced. He hadn't forgotten that Bud's brother, Ollie, had been one of the older boys who'd called him that in first grade. Unfortunately, Bud hadn't forgotten either. "Come on, let's go," he said to his friends. He took a step backward.

"Hold on, Towelman. Don't you and your buddies want to play superheroes with us?"

Suddenly Finch realized that Thorn had one hand behind his back. So did Bud. They each seemed to be jiggling something, but what? Sticks? Rocks? Lumps of dirt? His heart lurched around his chest as if it were looking for a way out.

Finch took another step backward. Then he heard the snickering. He looked behind him and saw kids gathering, waiting for something to happen.

"Uh-oh, the Hypnotizer got away," Thorn announced. "Why don't you super-guys save yourselves from Sodaman and Spraybuddy instead?"

He whipped out a can of soda from behind him. So did Bud. Before Finch could move, they popped the tabs and began spraying him and his friends.

The kids who had gathered to watch backed up a little. Some gasped. Some laughed.

"Hey, stop!" Finch threw an arm over his face. With the other he reached out blindly for Thorn. Elliott and Raj both tried to grab the can from Bud, but Bud aimed for their eyes.

"Have a drink, Towelman! You must be thirsty from chasing those bad guys." Thorn pulled Finch's arm from his face. "Come on—open your mouth!"

Kev was short, but he was solid as a bulldog—and just as feisty. He tried to charge Thorn, but Thorn turned the rest of his can on him. When they were out of soda, Bud and Thorn threw the cans on the ground. Snorting and stomping like wild horses, they ran away. The crowd of onlookers began to disband, too.

Finch rubbed the soda from his eyes. He gazed down at his dripping shirt. He looked at his spattered friends. He couldn't believe they'd let themselves get sucked into this.

"What happened to you dudes?" Mr. Burns exclaimed as he walked into the room. The guys were trying to dry themselves with paper towels they'd gotten from the bathroom dispenser.

"Spilled something on myself," Finch mumbled without looking up. His Justice League T-shirt—the one showing Superman, Batman, Spider-Man, the Green Hornet, and others—was covered with dark blotches.

"Soda can exploded," Rajiv added.

"An accident," Kevin mumbled.

"It was volcanic cola," Elliott muttered.

Mr. Burns shook his head. "First days can be tough. In the teachers' room at lunch today, someone accidentally called me Slip instead of Slope. Everyone laughed. It reminded me of this kid that always called me Slippy or Sloppy when I was your age. I never thought it was funny."

The guys darted looks at one another. They tried not to laugh. Fin could feel his ears getting red. Raj and Kev were shaking. Finally, Elliott erupted into giggles.

"Sorry, Mr. Burns," he croaked.

Mr. Burns shrugged. "Okay, so maybe it was funny." He grinned at the guys. "Why don't you come over to the Critter Corner? I'll introduce you to my friends."

The boys followed him to the tanks on the windowsill.

"This is Lima Bean," Mr. Burns said, pointing to a dark green turtle, "and these guys are the class goldfish. They haven't got names yet." He picked up a shaker and sprinkled some flakes onto the surface of the water.

"The way they vacuum up the chow, you should call one Hoover," Elliott suggested as the fishes' perfectly round mouths sucked in the food.

"Yeah, and the other one could be Eureka," Kev said. "That's the kind of vacuum we have."

Mr. Burns laughed. "Okay, Hoover and Eureka it is."

Finch's glance wandered over to the third tank.

Two shells were lying on the sandy bottom. Suddenly he realized that two beady black eyes were peeking at him from the brown-and-white spotted shell. They weren't eyes in a face, either. They were eyes on the ends of stalks!

He looked at the other shell, a larger, yellowish-tan one, more closely. Sure enough, another pair of eyes on stems was watching him. A claw edged out and sort of waved.

"Weird," Finch whispered.

"Those are hermit crabs," Mr. Burns told him. "I named them after my brothers. The smaller one is Anthony, and the larger one is Phillip." Suddenly the teacher got a big grin on his face. "Say, how would you guys like to be the class zookeepers?"

NO MERCY

Mimi opened the door with a ferret draped over each shoulder. "Mom's not home yet. She's meeting with a client, but she said she'll be back early in case we need to go out for school supplies."

Finch held his backpack in front of his chest, hoping she wouldn't notice his messed-up shirt. "I already have everything I need," he said, heading for his room.

"Hey, want a snack?"

Finch kept on going. "Why? You think it will make up for your sneaky little trick?"

"What are you talking about?" Mimi scrunched up her face.

"You're a crummy actress," Finch answered. He walked into his room and shut the door. He peeled off his stained shirt, threw it on the floor, and pulled on another one. From deep in his backpack, he hauled out his cape and dumped it into the trash can next to his desk. "Sorry, but you've got to go," he murmured.

He swung his bag onto the artificial arm his dad had attached to the wall as a hook. Mr. Mundy was a prosthetist—he made artificial arms and legs that were practically bionic. Finch loved to hang out with him in his lab, but his dad hadn't asked him to visit even once this summer. He'd been too busy.

There was a knock on the door to his room. "Fin? I made pizza bagels."

"You're trying to buy me off," Finch accused.

"Why would I want to do that?" Mimi sounded innocent. It only made Finch angrier.

"You know why!"

"Okay, then forget it."

Finch heard his sister stomp off. But the irresistible aroma of smoking cheese wafted under his door. In another moment he appeared in the kitchen.

"Where's Kelly?" he asked as he slid into a chair at the table.

"Who?"

"Doh! Kelly—your best friend." He grabbed a pizza bagel off a plate and took a big bite.

Mimi just shrugged. "How come you're so grouchy? Is your new teacher really mean and nasty?"

"Busted! I've got this new guy, Mr. Burns. He does yoga, plays the bugle, and reads to us. Today we started *The Indian in the Cupboard* about this boy who has a plastic Indian that comes alive."

"I read that when I was a kid," Mimi said.

"Correction—you're still a kid," Finch pointed out. "Anyway, Mr. Burns set up these learning centers around the room. One of them is the Critter Corner. And guess what—I'm a class zookeeper."

Mimi cast him a sideways glance. "You mean for real animals?"

"Doh! No, animal crackers! Of course they're real. There's a turtle, two goldfish, and two hermit crabs."

"You call that a zoo?"

Finch ignored the comment. "I'm in charge of the hermies."

"Hermit crabs—ew. They don't even have faces."

"That's prejudiced!" Finch objected. "You're prejudiced against animals without faces! Besides, they've got these cute little eyes on stems."

"Do they bite?"

"I don't think so. I'm going to look them up on the Internet."

"Maybe I'll do it with you."

There—he'd caught her. Mimi never wanted to hang out with him. "I knew it! I knew you were guilty!" Finch said, spraying food everywhere. "You put my cape in my backpack. You're trying to make me think I'm crazy!"

"You think I put your cape in your backpack? You know what, Fin? You really are crazy." Mimi got up and walked out of the kitchen.

Finch felt as if he had pizza stuck in his throat. Something was wrong. If Mimi really were guilty, she would be pressing him for all the humiliating details. He closed his eyes and remembered rushing about, tossing notebooks, pencils, a sweatshirt, and other stuff into his bag this morning. Was it possible he'd accidentally shoved the cape in, too?

A little part of him wondered if he should apologize. He sort of wished he could tell Mimi what had happened in the school yard. But he hated to admit she'd been right. She'd warned him about playing superheroes. It was his fault he'd gotten caught.

He left the rest of his pizza on the table and trudged back to his room. But when he got to the doorway, he stopped short. His superhero cape was floating around on the floor in an undulating motion, sort of the way a stingray did underwater. It was bumping into the trash can, the desk chair, and the floor lamp. Before he could squelch it, Fin let out a pizza burp. The cape seemed to hear the sound. It changed directions and began moving toward him.

"Whoa, get away!" Finch grabbed one of his books off the floor and held it like a weapon. But the cape only came toward him faster.

"Hey!"

The cape crashed into his legs. It squeaked. Finch plucked it up in two fingers. Cubby blinked his beady brown eyes up at him.

"Cubby, how many times have I told you to stay out of the garbage?" Finch scolded. He was about to drop the cape into the can again when something stopped him.

Please have mercy on an old friend.

Finch whapped his forehead with a palm. "Shut up!" he said aloud. His new, fourth-grade mind was becoming very annoying. He shut the door to his room anyway. One last time, he draped the old green bath towel over his shoulders and tied the strings at the neck. He gazed at himself in the mirror on his closet door. The cape used to look like a blanket on him. Now it was a better fit. It made him look taller and more dignified—like a combination of a superhero and a prince. He turned around to admire the yellow lightning bolts zigzagging across it.

Very dashing if I do say so myself, Master.

Fin froze. *Dashing* was a word like *repast*—a word he hadn't realized he knew. A cool breeze crept across his back. Suddenly he had the feeling he wasn't alone. Well, why couldn't his cape have magic powers like the ring in *The Lord of the Rings*, or the invisibility cloak in *Harry Potter*? He pictured himself wearing the cape to school and turning Thorn into a hermit crab with the wave of a hand.

He looked in the mirror again. This time all he saw was a skinny kid with sticky-out ears who was too old to be wearing a superhero costume. "Quit being a baby," he told his mirror self. He untied the strings, dumped the cape back in the garbage, and went to the computer room.

THE TATTLETALE FERRET

Finch Googled “hermit crabs” and found a site called Fun Facts About Hermit Crabs.

1. Hermit crabs have ten legs like shrimp.
2. Hermit crabs have two pairs of antennae. The longer pair is for feeling. The shorter pair is for smelling and tasting.
3. A hermit crab’s large claw is for defense. The small one is for feeding itself.
4. Hermit crabs don’t make the shells they live in—they find them.

5. Hermit crabs are most active at night.
6. Hermit crabs may fight over a shell. It is possible for an attacking crab to pull off the defending crab's claw if

"Mimi, Fin, I'm home!"

"Coming in a minute, Mom," Finch called. He bookmarked the Fun Facts website and dashed into the kitchen.

"Guess what? My teacher, Mr. Burns, picked me to be a class zookeeper."

"Nice." Finch's mother stepped out of her high heels and wriggled her toes. "Ooh, what a hard day."

"Did you sell any insurance policies?" Finch asked.

"Yep," Elaine Mundy said as she unloaded store-made roast chicken, potato salad, and coleslaw from a grocery bag. She was the most successful insurance saleswoman at the Safe and Sound Insurance Agency. Fin was very proud of her.

"My client Mrs. Fogel was worried about who would take care of her three dachshunds if she were no longer able. Her niece likes the dogs, but Mrs. Fogel didn't think the young woman could afford to look after them. So she bought an insurance policy that would provide her niece with enough money to take care of all three pups if she becomes incapacitated—or dies. Mrs. Fogel is in good shape, but she's quite old."

"Three dachshunds!" Mimi exclaimed as she shuffled into the room with Rosie attached to her fuzzy pink slipper. "Can we get another ferret?"

"Definitely not!" Mrs. Mundy exclaimed. "Two is the perfect number. Any more and this place will smell like a zoo. In fact, it already does—whose turn is it to clean the ferrets' litter box?"

Finch looked at the ceiling. "I don't smell anything."

"You never do," Mimi said, "because you're such a stinker."

"Fin, I want you to change that litter right after dinner," his mother said. "If you neglect your responsibilities in school like this, your teacher will take away your zoo job."

"Yeah, he'll let someone else clean the crab poop instead," Mimi teased.

"No, he won't! I'm going to take the best care of them ever," Finch shouted.

"Enough!" Mrs. Mundy commanded without looking away from the salad she was tossing. "Set the table." She waved a salad spoon in the air. "Why don't you two tell me how your first day of school went?"

Except for the scraping of spoon against bowl, the kitchen was silent.

Mrs. Mundy sighed. "That well, huh?"

"Are you and Kelly in any of the same classes?" Mrs. Mundy asked at dinner.

"Homeroom," Mimi muttered as she pushed her potato salad around her plate. "Math. Spanish."

"That's nice."

"No, it's not," Mimi said.

"I thought Kelly was your best friend," Finch mumbled with his mouth full. Bits of coleslaw dribbled down his chin.

"Not anymore. I hate Kelly! She told everyone I like Ollie Rosebud."

Finch dropped his fork. "Yuck. He's a creep. "

Mimi stared at her fork as if she'd never seen one before. "No, he's not. I do like him."

"Ollie *Rosebud*—are you crazy?" Finch yelled. "He's the one who teased me about my cape in first grade."

Mimi snorted. "First grade? Get over it."

That only got Finch more worked up. "His brother, Bud, is friends with the worst kid in class. The two of them hate me!" Finch was on the verge of telling his mother and sister about Sodaman and Spraybuddy. He needed to know what to do if it happened again.

But before he got the chance, his mother said, "Fin, you're not helping." Then she turned to Mimi. "Maybe Kelly was trying to do you a favor. Maybe now you'll find out Ollie likes you, too."

"No, Mom, you don't understand!" Mimi wailed. "Ollie already has a girlfriend—Holly Taylor—the most popular girl in class. Kelly just wanted to embarrass me to get on Holly's good side."

Blah, blah, blah, blah. Finch stopped listening. He concentrated on trying to lift the blue bowl of coleslaw with his mind, but it remained in the center of the table. He put his fork on his lap and tried to bend it without using his hands, but he couldn't make a dent. He attempted to make his chair fly around the room, but it wouldn't move. He sighed loudly but no one noticed.

Swish . . . swish . . . swish . . . swish. A strange noise came from outside the room. That got everyone's attention. It sounded like someone was mopping the floor. In another moment, a gray cloth appeared at the entrance to the kitchen. Rosie was dragging it.

Finch jumped out of his chair. "Rosie, give me that!"

But Mimi leaned down and got it first. "Let me see, baby," she said as she took the rag away from the ferret. "Ew, what is this?"

Finch jumped up. He tried to snatch it from his sister, but his mother caught his arm. "Isn't that your Justice League T-shirt, Finch? What happened?"

Finch swallowed. "Why don't you ask Ollie Rosebud's brother? Spraybuddy!"

THE CRAB THAT FLEW

Finch was finishing his cereal when his mother appeared in the kitchen. "What are you doing down here so early?" she asked.

"I want to get to school before class starts so I can do my job. Would you drop me off on the way to work?"

Mrs. Mundy squinted her left eye the way she always did when she was doubtful about something. "I have to meet a client at eight. Won't you be too early?"

"Some of the teachers will be there. I can sit in the corridor and read if the classroom door is locked."

But the door to the classroom was open, and Mr. Burns was at his computer when Finch arrived.

"Hi, Mr. Burns. I wanted to get started with my zookeeper job, if it's okay."

"Sure, Fin—good idea. It will take the hermies a while to get used to you. They may not come out of their shells until they feel they can trust you."

"Okay." Finch went over to the table and stared into the tank. The crab in the small white shell with brown spots was hunkered down in a corner. "Hey, Anthony," he said quietly.

The crab in the larger shell poked out its eye-stalks. With its small claw it reached up and tapped the tank. Maybe it was crab-talk for "I'm hungry." Fin reached for the jar called Hermit Crab Grub on the tray beside the tank. While he was reading the feeding instructions, his classmates started arriving. Some of them wandered over to the Critter Corner.

"Excuse me, I'm one of the zookeepers." Elliott elbowed through the kids and stood next to Finch. Kevin and Rajiv squeezed up to the table, too.

Raj reached for the turtle food. "I'll take care of Lima Bean."

"I'll feed Hoover and you feed Eureka," Elliott told Kev.

"You can't feed one fish at a time," Kev said. "You can't even tell them apart."

"Sure I can. I'm already an expert on them," El replied. "For instance, do you know why goldfish are orange?"

"No, why?" Chloe and Kayla asked from behind the boys.

Elliott peered over his shoulder and grinned. "Because the water makes them rusty."

"Uhh," Kev grunted. But Chloe and Kayla both giggled.

"Boy, that stuff stinks," Bud announced as Fin unscrewed the top to the hermit-crab food.

"Then why don't you go somewhere else?" Finch sprinkled the food into the crabs' dish. Phil stuck his legs out of his shell. His antennae twitched. But Anthony didn't move at all.

"Come on, Anthony, it's your breakfast, too." Finch lifted the lid on the tank and picked up the smaller crab. "It's okay, boy, I'm your friend," he murmured as he held it on a flat, steady palm.

Suddenly it seemed as if the entire class was in the

Critter Corner, pushing and shoving to get closer to the tanks.

"Let me see!"

"Can I hold him?"

"Gimme." A hand snatched Anthony off Finch's palm.

Finch whirled around.

"What's the matter, Towelman?" Thorn jeered. "Did you lose your little super-crabby?" He raised his fist.

"Don't hold him like that!" Finch snapped. "You'll scare him."

"Scare him? It's just a stupid crab. It doesn't have feelings."

"Give him back!" Finch grabbed Thorn's arm.

Thorn shoved Finch away. *Bam!* Finch fell back against the table. Water sloshed out of the goldfish tank. Elliott threw his arms around it to steady it.

Finch launched himself toward Thorn. "Give me that crab!" But Thorn stuck his arm straight up so that the fist that held Anthony was out of Finch's reach.

Finch leaped for the fist and stumbled forward. As he came down, his hand whacked Thorn on the nose.

"Oooooooh!" his classmates gasped.

Flaaah! Flaaah! Flaaaaaaah! Mr. Burns blew his

bugle so hard everyone jumped. Thorn's hand sprang open.

"Nooo!" Finch cried as Anthony flew through the air. He felt a thump on the top of his sneaker. He looked down. Anthony was resting there.

"Everyone freeze!"

While the kids stood like statues, Mr. Burns strode over to the Critter Corner. He leaned down in front of Finch and scooped Anthony up.

"Is he okay?" Finch asked.

Mr. Burns brought his palm up to eye level. "I think so. Landing on the sneaker probably saved him—no thanks to you boys."

"Me? But it wasn't my fault—" Finch began.

"Yes, it was." Thorn sniffled. "You socked me and I dropped him. I couldn't help it." Blood was leaking out of his nose.

"I didn't!" Finch protested. "I fell."

"You'd better go to the nurse's office and get some ice for that nosebleed," Mr. Burns told Thorn.

Bud bounced on his toes. "Should I go with him?"

Mr. Burns hesitated a moment. "No."

Finch touched his teacher's arm to get his attention. "Mr. Burns, it really wasn't my fault. I didn't mean to—"

But Mr. Burns cut him off. "I don't want to hear it. I'll talk to you later during recess. For now, just go back to your seat."

"You didn't even see what happened," Finch protested.

"I said later, Fin." Mr. Burns turned away. "Everyone—return to your desks and take out your math books."

After lunch, Finch went back to the classroom instead of out to the school yard with the rest of the guys. Mr. Burns was reading a magazine called *Snowboarder*.

"Don't sit at your desk, Finch. Come over to the rug." Mr. Burns closed his magazine. "I thought we could do a little yoga together. Before we begin, I want you to know something. Yoga is not a punishment. That's not why you're here. Doing yoga stretches not only the body, but the mind, too. It can help you think clearly and have more positive thoughts. And it's a great way to chill out."

Mr. Burns lowered himself down easily and sat Indian-style. Finch plopped down and slouched over. He breathed a noisy sigh. Maybe yoga wasn't a punishment, but what about losing your recess time?

"Anyone can fight," Mr. Burns said as quietly as if

he were telling Finch a secret. "But bullying isn't the answer. The thinking person figures out a better way to solve a problem."

Finch clenched his jaw. Mr. Burns was going to make a terrible teacher. He couldn't even tell a bully from a victim. He still hadn't heard Finch's side of the story. It was as if he didn't care who was right.

But in a few moments, Finch was in the downward-facing dog pose. He was bent over at the middle with his hands and feet on the floor. His arms and legs were stretched out tight. His rear end was pointed up in the air. The pose was harder to do than it looked, but Finch tried until he got it.

"Not bad," Mr. Burns said. "Now let's try the rattlesnake pose—and if we have time, we'll do the scorpion."

Finch thought Scorpionman would be a good name for a superhero—or an evil villain. There were times when it would be extremely helpful to have a poisonous stinger. Like right now. *Zap!* He'd use it on Thorn. It was his fault Mr. Burns didn't like Fin after just a day and a half of school.

The thought created a stinging feeling behind Fin's eyes. He kept his head down. He wondered if he would ever be able to change his teacher's mind.

THE BEGINNING

Finch was down on the floor of his room, leaning on his forearms and his right knee. His left leg was in the air, knee bent, toes pointed up at the ceiling. It was a version of the scorpion pose, although he hadn't totally gotten it yet. He still needed to raise his right knee off the floor too, balancing on his foot instead. He was determined to be ready in case Mr. Burns asked him to do yoga again. He wanted his teacher to see he'd been practicing.

One, two, three, up! He pushed onto the ball of his foot, toppled over, and hit his head on the garbage

can. "Ow! Ow!" he moaned as he lay there rubbing his temple.

Cubby scampered in to check out the commotion. He climbed over Fin's face and headed for the garbage can, which had rolled onto its side.

Pfu! Pfu! Get off of me, you odiferous polecat!

Finch let out a giggle. Now the mind voice was being funny. He wondered if he'd gotten a concussion or if he was going a little crazy.

He reached into the can and pulled Cubby out. Then he removed the cape. He had to admit he was glad the old thing was still in the garbage. After the day he'd had, he needed something to calm him down and help him think clearly. He folded it into a pillow and stuck it under his head.

It was a joke that Mr. Burns had gotten mad at him for fighting today, but not the ha-ha kind of joke. It had been the only time in his entire life that he'd hit someone. Once again, he saw his hand smacking Thorn's nose and bright red blood snaking from Thorn's nostrils. Ugg. Fin was sure Thorn would find a way to get even.

In comic books, superheroes always did a lot of fighting. There were tons of *kapows!* and *kapops!* But if he was ever to be a real superhero, Fin thought he'd have to be a different kind.

"Yeah, right," he told himself.

But an idea had already begun stirring his brain—no, his entire body—into action. He sprang up off the floor and headed for his desk, stopping to grab the cape off the floor. It might help to think like a superhero, he told himself as he tied it on. Then he dropped into his desk chair and began writing.

The Oath

I PROMISE to do my best to help others at all times.

Ugg. That sounded like the Boy Scout oath. Finch had been a Cub Scout for a few months. At the first den meeting, he'd made a compass out of a penny and a paper clip. At another, he'd made a mini-tepee out of brown paper and Popsicle sticks. And at his third and last, he'd carved a canoe out of a bar of soap. But he'd wanted real compasses, real tents, and real boats! He'd refused to go to another meeting, even after his mother pointed out how much she'd spent on the uniform.

I PROMISE to do my best to help others at all times, to fight only for truth and justice, never for selfish or evil ends.

There—that was better. Sure, he'd borrowed a bit from Superman's oath, but he didn't think the big guy would mind. Something else was missing, though. He chewed on one of the cape strings while he considered what it was.

I PROMISE to do my best to help others at all times, to fight only for truth and justice, never for selfish or evil ends, but to solve problems by thinking, not fighting, whenever I can.

Hmmm . . . the last part sounded like something Mr. Burns would say. But Fin liked the idea anyway—especially when he thought of Thorn's sickeningly bloody nose.

As a member of the Super Secret Heroes' Club,

No, that sounded like kindergarten. Fin chewed the end of his pen.

As a member of the Super Secret Heroes' Association,

No, that sounded like a group of businessmen.

Perchance you should try "Society."

Finch pressed his palm against his forehead. He wished the mind voice would go away already. Still, he liked the sound of it—the Society of Super Secret Heroes.

As a member of the Society of Super Secret Heroes, I will carry out all missions without ever letting anyone know that it was me. I will protect the Thinking Cape from falling into the hands of ordinary people. And most of all, I will keep my true identity hidden and the SSSh a secret until I die.

Fin put down his pen.

He read the Oath aloud in a low, quick mumble. "The Thinking Cape? Come on!" he chided himself as he crossed that part out. He gazed over the paper once more and covered his eyes with a hand. "What

The Oath

I PROMISE to do my best to help others at all times, to fight only for truth and justice, never for selfish or evil ends, but to solve problems by thinking, not fighting, whenever I can. As a member of the Society of Super Secret Heroes, I will carry out all missions without ever letting anyone know that it was me. ~~I will protect the Thinking Cape from falling into the hands of ordinary people~~. And most of all, I will keep my identity hidden and the SSSh a secret until I die.

am I doing?" he moaned. "I can't show this to the guys. They'll think the whole thing is stupid."

On the contrary, it is the finest oath I have ever heard.

This was sick! Now the mind voice was answering him. "Shut up!" he snapped.

Yes, Master Fin.

Finch froze. "Wh—who are you?"

I am the Thinking Cape.

Quickly, Fin untied the cape from his neck and threw it into the wastebasket. He needed to go to a doctor right away.

Have I displeased you, Master?

"You're just some old cloth. You can't speak," he said.

You are right, Master. No common cape can speak. But I am not common.

Finch pressed his hands against his temples. This only happened in books or movies. It couldn't be real. "I'm not actually hearing anything," he told himself firmly.

It is true that you are not hearing me with your ears. You are hearing me with your mind, Master.

"Stop calling me that!"

I am sorry, but I cannot help myself. It is part of the

rules. When you guessed my identity, you became my master.

"What identity?"

But I have told you. I am the Thinking Cape. That is what you called me when you put me on and wrote the Oath.

"It's not a real oath. I was just fooling around," Fin said.

It could be real, Master. My job is to help make ordinary mortals into extraordinary ones. I can assist you in following the Oath—to do your best to help others. You do want to be a real superhero, do you not?

Maybe I'm dreaming, Finch thought. How else could I be talking to my kindergarten plaything? How else could it be answering back? "I don't really like fighting," he answered finally. "I can't stand the sight of blood."

Rest assured I detest violence as well. I can help you solve problems by thinking, not fighting. That is my power, Master.

"I AM NOT YOUR MASTER!" Fin shouted.

Alas, there is nothing to be done about it. The rules cannot be changed. O Master, you have no idea what a relief this is! I have been waiting a thousand years.

"No! I don't want to be a mental case." Fin picked

up the wastebasket. "I'm dumping you into the garbage can by the driveway. You can talk to the trash from now on."

But Master, should you not ask the other members of the Society of Super Secret Heroes what they think first? Perchance they would appreciate having a magical cape.

"There aren't any other members. There isn't any Society of Super Secret Heroes."

Do you not think your friends would like to be members—and superheroes? You could ask them to join you.

Fin hesitated. "My friends could hear you, too?"

Of course—if you want them to.

Finch thought about how amazed the guys would be if they heard the Thinking Cape speak in their heads. They'd freak out, of course. But if they heard it, too, that would mean he wasn't nuts. He had to know.

"All right. Maybe tomorrow, I'll ask the guys to come over. But don't talk to me anymore until then."

Yes, Master.

"I said no talking!" Finch shoved the cape to the bottom of his backpack. This time the Thinking Cape didn't answer.

On Wednesday nights, Finch and Mimi always had dinner with their father—unless Mr. Mundy had to babysit for Jake. The kid was eight months old now. Sometimes Finch's dad brought him to see Jake, but the little blob had a schedule like a business executive. It was always time for his lunch, his bath, his nap, his walk, his playgroup, his baby gym class, or his baby swim class. Mostly, Finch saw the back of the kid's head as he was leaving. It was hard to feel brotherly.

Tonight they went to Finch's favorite Italian restaurant, Sal's, since Mimi claimed she was too sick to go out. They sat in their favorite booth, which was next to a window in the wall where you could watch the two pizza men, Dom and Louie, tossing pies. Sometimes Finch and his father bet on which of the guys would finish making a pizza first. Or else they tried to guess what toppings would go on the next pie. But tonight, Finch just stared through the window while he downed a soda.

"A pepperoni for your thoughts," his father said.

"Dad, when you were a kid, were you normal?"

"Normal? I don't know, Fin. One man's normal is another man's nuts."

"What?"

Fin's dad grinned. "I mean it's normal for people to have different opinions of what's normal."

Finch twisted his straw wrapper between his fingers. His father wasn't helping. "I don't think I'm normal," he blurted out.

"In what way?"

Finch hesitated. What if his dad whisked him off to the hospital? But he had to tell someone. He couldn't take it anymore. "I've been hearing this voice in my head."

"What does it say?"

Finch felt his ears getting hot. "It reminds me of stuff. And, um, I think it wants me to be a superhero."

"That sounds exciting."

"Dad!"

Mr. Mundy smiled. "Sorry. So it's like you're talking to yourself?"

"Sort of—but not exactly. It's more like someone else is talking."

"Who?"

"I'm not exactly sure," Fin said after a long sip of his soda.

Mr. Mundy nodded. "You know, I used to be a lot

like you. Except, I used to think about robots instead of super-guys. I wanted to invent one that would do homework, take out the trash, rake the leaves, and be my friend. Every year for science fair, I made a robot. I liked to imagine it could talk to me—but the most I could ever get it to do was pick up a golf ball. One Halloween, I dressed up in a robot costume. After that the kids called me Robo-boy."

Finch imagined his dad in a costume made of foil-covered cardboard boxes from the supermarket. It wasn't a pretty sight. But it made him decide to trust his father. He took a deep breath and let it out slowly. "Dad? I think I know who—I mean what—the voice is."

Mr. Mundy was looking at his watch. "Hold on, Fin. I've got to make a quick call to Lisa. Jakey has an ear infection. I want to make sure the pain isn't back. Then you can tell me more, okay?" He took out his cell phone without waiting for an answer.

Finch turned back to the window. One of the pizza men, Dom, grinned at him, but he was too upset to smile back. His dad didn't really care about his problems. He'd only been pretending to be interested in what Fin had been saying. Probably, he'd been thinking about Jake the whole time.

Anyway, it had been a bad idea to tell his father about the voice, Finch chided himself. No adult would take him seriously. He began making loud slurping sounds with his straw. He kicked the back of the booth with his heels. The people at the next table glared at him.

"I've got to go now, Lisa," Mr. Mundy said quickly. "I'll be home soon." He snapped his phone shut and looked across the table at Fin. "So, about the voice. You were going to tell me what you think it is."

Fin shrugged. "I guess it's just my imagination," he mumbled.

When Sal brought their pizza to the table, he gobbled down his slices. He wanted to get home fast so he could call the guys. They were his only hope.

TILL DEATH DO US PART

"Until I die?" Elliott dropped the paper from his fingers.

The guys were sitting in a circle on the floor of Fin's room, passing the Oath around. The ferrets crawled in and out of their laps, sniffing for raisins and crumbs. Fin finished tying on the cape and lifted Cubby into his arms. He hadn't mentioned anything about the Thinking Cape yet. He knew his friends would never believe it could talk unless they heard it themselves. But now that they were all together, he wasn't sure how to begin. What if he'd been imagining the whole thing—if he really was crazy?

"Why does it have to be a 'secret' society?" Elliott complained. "If I'm going to be doing good, why can't I let anyone know?"

"Remember the gift or the curse?" Finch asked. "Superheroes never reveal their true identities. Otherwise people would always be bothering them to do things. They'd never get any rest."

"Besides, if anyone found out about the Society, we'd be goners. We'd have to move to Reject Island," Raj explained, as if he were talking to his little brother. "I mean it El, you wouldn't be able to tell anyone!"

"Okay, okay." Elliott held up a hand like a policeman stopping traffic. "We'll be super secret heroes."

"Yeah—except we haven't got the super part," Kevin pointed out. "How can we be superheroes without superpowers?"

"We'd be a different type of superhero—the regular person kind. But maybe we'd have, er, outside help," Fin said.

"Yeah? Who's going to help us—Batman?" Kev asked. "You got his cell number?"

Raj and El burst out laughing.

Finch swallowed. So far, the only thing talking inside him was his nervous stomach. "Come on, say something," he urged in his head. But the Thinking Cape didn't make a peep.

"I've got superpowers," Elliott announced. "I'm Elliott the Elastic."

"Funny," Kev said in a bored voice.

"No really, I—AHH . . . AHH . . ." Elliott reared back and let out a huge sneeze. "ACHOOO!" A string of greenish-yellow snot shot out of his nose and dangled all the way to the floor.

"Yeeeuck!" Raj and Kev scrambled backward.

Elliott pounded his chest with a fist. "See? Even my snot is elastic!" He reached out a finger and plucked the strand like a guitar string.

"Hey, that's rubber snot!" Raj exclaimed.

"Yep, my newest gag from Gag-o-Rama," Elliott said. Carefully, he wound up the snot and stuffed it into his cargo pocket.

"I think Fin's idea is cool," Raj said when the guys had settled down. "I wouldn't mind being a secret superhero. I could be Raj the Remarkable. That's what I'm going to call myself when I become a professional magician."

Kev snorted. "So we're all supposed to have secret names?"

"Why not? Yours can be Kev the Killjoy," Elliott said.

Fin and Raj cracked up.

"Ha-ha. You're not funny," Kev said, but he looked like he was trying not to smile. He pulled a marker and a little pad from his pocket and began doodling something.

Elliott reached over and tugged the edge of the cape. "Hey, Fin, why did you cross out the part in the Oath about the Thinking Cape? It's an excellent name. It could be our mascot."

"Yeah, like the funny ones all the sports teams have," Kev agreed. "Did you ever see the Padres' giant chicken or the Mighty Ducks' wacky quacker?"

Foolish fowl! Preposterous poultry! I do not want to be a mascot, Master!

There it was. Finch glanced around at the guys to see if they'd heard anything. Raj was pulling on his ear. Elliott was shaking his head. Kevin was feeling his forehead.

"Mascots are for sports teams," Fin murmured. "And they're usually kind of silly. The Thinking Cape is more like a symbol." He stared into his lap.

"I was just thinking that," Raj said slowly.

Kev shot him a sideways glance. "So was I."

"Me, too," Elliott whispered.

Finch gathered up his courage. "Did any of you hear, er, a voice say 'foolish fowl' or 'preposterous poultry'?"

The guys all looked at one another. Each gave a tiny nod.

"Only, not out loud," Raj said quietly. "I heard it in my head." He turned to Finch. "Was it inside yours, too?"

Fin nodded. He couldn't get any words out.

"I thought my head was haunted!" Elliott exclaimed. "The voice said, 'I do not want to be a mascot, Master!'" He shot Fin a sideways glance. "Did it mean you?"

Indeed I did, Elliott the Elastic. Master Finch is the first person to have guessed my identity in a thousand years. He wrote it down: "the Thinking Cape." That is the reason I can finally speak again. Now he is my master.

For a moment, the guys just stared at one another. Then Kev thumped Raj on the back. "Ha-ha. This is your new magic trick, right—ventriloquism?"

"No ventriloquist can throw his voice inside someone's head," Raj whispered.

Elliott eyeballed the ceiling. "Then . . . who's doing the talking?"

As I said before, it is I who speaks—the Thinking Cape.

Fin's brain was racing. If everyone heard the voice, then he wasn't nuts! "It's true—it can talk," he said. He untied the cape and placed it in the middle of the floor. "At least I think it can. I've been hearing it in my head for days."

Raj stared. "You've been hearing voices?"

Finch gulped. "Only this voice. I asked the Thinking Cape to let you hear it, too."

"G-gee, thanks," Kev stammered.

"Get it to say something else, Fin," Elliott urged. "You're its master."

Finch leaned forward. He felt kind of foolish. "Um, Cape?"

Yes, Master Finch. How may I be of help?

"Can you do our homework?" Elliott asked before Fin could think of a reply.

Nay, Elliott the Elastic, that is not possible, I'm afraid.

"Can you bring us a trunk full of money?" Kev asked.

Nay, Kev the Killjoy, that is not possible either.

"Then what can you do?" Raj asked.

You see, Raj the Remarkable, my job is to help make ordinary mortals into extraordinary ones. I can assist you in becoming superheroes.

"Yeah, right. There's got to be a microphone in here somewhere," Kev said as he crawled around peering under the furniture. The rest of the guys began searching, too. Raj poked under Fin's pillows and Elliott looked in the trash can. Even Finch looked under the bed, although he knew he wouldn't find anything.

Finally Raj said, "Who are we kidding? Even if there were a microphone, how could it speak inside our minds?"

No one could come up with an answer.

Elliott leaned toward the cape. "Are you from outer space?"

Nay, Elliott the Elastic.

Elliott giggled. "Could you just call me Elliott?"

As you wish, Elliott.

"You already know I got the cape from a garage sale, El," Fin said.

"Yeah, I remember." Kev poked the cape. "So if you're really magic, what were you doing there?"

I am afraid that is a long, sad story, Kev the Killjoy.

"Call me Kev," Kev grunted. "Let's hear the story."

"Hold on. First everyone needs to sign the Oath," Finch said. He held out his pen. One by one, the boys signed their names. No one said a word until Fin finished putting it away in his desk.

"Okay, Cape," he said solemnly, "the Society of Super Secret Heroes is officially ready."

For a long time, I was forced to be a lowly towel. But that was not the way my life began. My cotton was grown in a special field that belonged to a family of cape makers. The cloaks they made were the most prized in the kingdom, for it was known that they had extraordinary powers.

"Where was your kingdom?" Raj asked.

A thousand years ago the borders were not so clear. It might have been Persia, or Arabia, or India. But perchance you know that the world has changed, Raj the Remarkable.

"You can call me Raj," Raj said. "But what was the name of the kingdom?" He squinted as if he were trying to see the place.

My home was Gizli Yer. It means Secret Earth.

"Quit interrupting it, Raj," Elliott complained. He

reached out and stroked the green cape like a pet. "So what happened to you?"

I was purchased from the cape makers' shop by a man who traveled from kingdom to kingdom buying and selling goods. With me across his shoulders, the trader strutted like a peacock, enjoying the compliments he received on my fine fabric and golden strings. My master often asked my advice on business dealings, and with my help, his wealth grew great. Unfortunately, he was never satisfied. One day, he did not like the answer I gave to a problem he asked me to solve.

"What was the problem?" Kev asked.

He wanted me to tell him how to steal grain from his neighbor's storage shed without getting caught. But we capes are supposed to work for good, not evil. I merely pointed out that since he was too fat already, he did not need more grain.

The boys snickered.

Unfortunately, my owner flew into a fury. He shouted that I would be more useful as a towel and ordered a maid to take me to the bathhouse. But first, he cut off my golden strings. Without them, I could no longer speak. In time, it was forgotten that I was ever a cape at all. Oh, how my fibers quiver to think of all the generations that have dried themselves on me.

"You still haven't said how you got to the garage sale," Finch reminded it. He stretched his arms and wiggled his toes. The Thinking Cape sure could talk.

I was getting to that, Master Finch. Since magic cotton such as mine never wears out, I was passed down from one relative to another. I was living in the linen closet of a family not far away, when the mother of the house decided to make me into a costume for her son. She gave me green satin strings and sewed on my lightning bolts. But her ungrateful brat refused to wear me. He said he wished to be Batman—whoever that is. That is why I ended up in the garage sale among the other unwanted items.

"If you hadn't spoken for a thousand years, how come you can speak now?" Kev asked.

When the brat's mother sewed my new strings on, a surprising thing happened. I began to sense my voice returning.

Elliott ran one of the strings through his fingers. "Did you try to talk to her or the brat?"

Nay, Elliott. It is against the rules. I am only permitted to speak with those who know my true identity. Besides, I could not bear having the brat as a master.

"Do you ever talk out loud, Cape?" Raj asked.

Never. For me it is not possible.

"Too bad. If people could hear you, you could go on TV. You'd be famous," Elliott said.

Suddenly, from outside Fin's door, something began roaring. It sounded like a vacuum cleaner. "That's funny. It's not Gloria's day," he said. Gloria was the Mundys' cleaning lady. She only came on Fridays.

"Maybe somebody's here to steal the cape," Raj whispered. Just then, something bumped hard against the door. The guys jumped.

Finch stood up and tiptoed over to it. Slowly, he reached for the knob.

"Be careful," Elliott hissed.

The thing crashed against the door again—harder this time. Finch took a deep breath and cracked it open.

FINCH FLIPS OUT

Blaaam! A vacuum cleaner hurtled through the opening, followed by Fin's sister.

"Hey! What are you doing?" he protested.

"What does it look like?" Mimi shouted over the noise. With furious strokes, she shoved the vacuum back and forth across the floor. Rosie and Cubby flew out of the room like furry demons. Finch snatched up the Oath just before the vacuum swallowed it. Raj, Kev, and Elliott jumped onto the bed.

"Pick up your feet!" Mimi ordered them.

They swung their legs off the floor.

"Who do you think you are—Gloria?" Finch shouted. "Go clean somewhere else."

"We don't need a cleaning lady!" Mimi yelled over the vacuum's roar. "It's time you stopped being so spoiled. We need to save money so I can go to private school."

"I've got an idea! You should go to boarding school. If you do, I'll give you all the money in my college bank account," Finch said with a big grin on his face.

The guys smirked, but Mimi didn't think it was so funny. "Boarding school? You want me to live away from home?" She chased Fin with the vacuum nozzle. It swept up the cape and began sucking it in.

Aiyyya! Help me!

Finch grabbed the vacuum cord and

pulled it out of the wall. Instantly, the noise stopped. "GET OUT!" he screamed at his sister.

"All right, I'll go. But you'd better dust this place. You can use this old rag." Mimi tossed him the cape. "I warn you—I'm coming back to check." She dragged the vacuum out of the room. Finch kicked the door shut after her.

"Oh, man! What got into her?" Raj whispered.

Finch shook his head. "I don't know. She's been acting weirder than usual lately."

Elliott looked at his watch. "Oops—time to go. My mom is coming home early tonight."

Kev stood up. "I'd better go, too. I promised I'd clean my room today."

"I should help my grandma with the twins. They've been really bad lately," Raj said. He put a hand on Fin's shoulder.

"But you can't leave me here with the, er, you-know-what," Finch protested.

"Why not? You're its master," Elliott said.

"Besides, it's always lived here," Kev added.

Fin felt a lump growing in his throat. "But everything is different now. Maybe I should tell my mom or dad about it."

"No! They'll take it away from us," Elliott exclaimed.

"But what if I can't take care of it?" Fin said. "I'm messy. I make mistakes. I forget things. What if I leave it somewhere?"

I do not think that will happen, Master. I trust you. Besides, I do not want to belong to an adult.

"Why not?"

I wish to have fun for a change.

"Yay!" Elliott started clapping.

Fin ignored him. "But you could choose anyone you want to live with—like a billionaire or the president of the United States."

Billionaires and presidents would be disappointed with me, Master. After so many years of disuse, my power is as weak as the legs on a newborn camel. I am sorry, but if you try to give me away, I will not speak. The adults will think you are imagining things. I will be sent back to the closet—or worse.

"The cape is right," Kev agreed. "It would never have any fun if adults found out about it. Grown-ups aren't good at keeping secrets. It would be on the TV news and then people would try to steal it. Or else scientists would want to do tests on it. It would be locked up forever."

"Come on, Fin—don't you want to be extraordinary?" El begged.

Yes, please, Master! I have already spent centuries in closets and trunks. I could not bear it again!

"Okay, don't worry. I won't tell anyone," Fin said hoarsely. "None of us will, right?"

The guys all murmured agreement.

"Here." Kev tore out the page he'd been drawing on and handed it to Fin. It showed the letters SSSh with a lightning bolt running through them. "I made an emblem for us." He grinned. "And for the mascot, too."

"Thanks—it's really good," Fin said. He followed the guys to the front door and watched them hurry down the walk. He could tell they were glad to be going. Finding out about the cape had scared them, too. It wasn't like in books and movies where kids discovered unearthly creatures or found magic stuff. Those kids didn't get freaked out about their discoveries. He'd never realized how brave they were—or how unreal.

He trudged back to his room.

"Hi, Cape," he whispered as he closed the door.

Hello, Master Finch. How may I help you?

"Well, I was just wondering something. Can you always hear my thoughts?"

Nay. Your thoughts are shielded from me unless you want me to hear them. It is automatic.

Finch felt greatly relieved. He didn't want to have anyone listening to his thoughts all the time, even if that someone was a cape. He was pretty sure he didn't want to hear the cape talking all the time, either. "What if I left you home sometimes? Would I be able to hear you in school?"

Nay, Master. My voice would not carry over such a distance. But if you grow tired of hearing me talk, you do not have to leave me behind. Just say, "Pell-mell, a speechless spell!" Then I must be quiet.

Another good feature! Finch thought. To his delight, the Thinking Cape didn't seem to detect his comment. The automatic thought shield was definitely working.

"Great!" he said. "Do you want to watch a superhero DVD now? I've got a Batman and a Spider-Man."

Excuse me, Master Finch, but aren't you going to ask how to end the speechless spell?

"Oh, sure."

You must say, "Quell, quell the speechless spell!" Then I will be able to speak again.

"Okay."

My last master said I talk too much. Do you think so?

"No," Finch replied, although it did seem pretty gabby. Once again, he was grateful for the thought shield.

Master Fin? I do have a request.

Finch swallowed. "What?"

Would you please tell me what a DVD is?

CORNERED!

Finch packed his book bag as quickly as he could and ran downstairs. His mom had agreed to drop him off again. She thought he wanted to be early because of his job as a crab keeper. But the truth was he felt as if he'd rather be at school than home alone with the cape. Besides, he needed to finish his math homework. Last night he'd been too antsy to concentrate on it.

Mr. Burns was standing on his head when Fin peeked into the classroom. Quietly, he backed away from the door. He didn't want to have to stand on his head, do the downward-facing dog, or admit that he hadn't finished his math assignment. For safety's sake, he decided to do it in the stairwell. As he walked down the hallway, he passed the teachers' room. The door was propped open. He took a quick look and saw his last year's teacher, Mrs. Rooney, getting coffee with Mrs. Goldstein, the school nurse.

Mrs. Goldstein waved. "Hi, Finny. How's the new baby brother?"

"He's okay—he's not so new anymore," Finch said. Mrs. Goldstein had been calling him Finny since kindergarten. He wished she'd stop.

"Did you and your buddies write any more *Super Ferrets* comics this summer?" Mrs. Rooney asked.

"We're almost finished with one."

"Well, bring it into my classroom when it's done. I'm sure the third graders would love to see it," Mrs. Rooney said.

"Okay," Finch agreed, although he wondered if they'd ever work on it again.

He passed the double doors of the gym next. The lights were on and he could hear the echoing sound of voices and the thudding of a ball. He glanced through the window in the door. The gym teacher, Mr. Fisher, was shooting baskets with the principal, Mr. Kutler, and Mr. Lacy, who taught the kids in special ed class. The three men often hung out together.

Fin pushed open the door to the stairwell and sat on the top step. He wondered if Mr. Burns played basketball. Come to think of it, he hadn't seen Mr. Burns talk to any of the teachers yet. Maybe it was because he was shy. Or it could be because he was new. He wondered if being a new teacher at school was like being a new student. No one ever rushed up to welcome them. They just had to try not to stick out until they weren't so new anymore.

Fin reached into his bag for his math book and felt the soft cloth of the Thinking Cape. His heart jumped—he still wasn't used to it. But the cape was quiet. They'd stayed up late watching the movie. Probably it was sleeping now. Fin was tired, too, but he had no time for napping. He still had to take care of the hermies. He raced through the homework and hurried back down the hall toward his classroom.

Just as he was passing the boys' room, the door opened. Two hands seized him.

"Hey!"

Finch was trying to struggle free when a second pair of arms shot out and grabbed him, too. In a moment, he was pulled inside.

"You didn't think you were going to get away with hitting me, did you, Towelman?"

"It was an accident," Finch said as Thorn pushed him up against the tiled wall. "I tripped. Your nose just got in the way. Besides, Mr. Burns already punished me. It's over."

"Oh, I'm not punishing you. You're just going to have another accident," Thorn said. "Only this time your nose is going to run into my fist."

"Yeah, an accident!" Bud echoed as he leaned against the bathroom door to keep anyone else from coming in.

Finch tried to squirm away, but Thorn only pushed him harder against the wall. His hand was right below Fin's neck, pressing his collarbone so hard he had to fight back tears of pain.

Tell them you will fight later, Master. Say you promised Mr. Burns you would arrive early.

At the sound of the cape's voice in his head, Finch took a breath. "I don't have time to fight now," he said, trying to sound calm. "I've got to finish feeding the crabs or they'll get crabby. I'll fight you later."

Thorn squinted into Finch's eyes. His hands let up a little.

"Besides, someone's going to want to go to the bathroom," Finch continued quickly. "If they can't get in, they'll call Mr. Paul. We'll all get in trouble." Mr. Paul was the custodian.

Thorn dropped his arms. "All right."

All right? Finch pulled down his T-shirt. He couldn't believe Thorn had agreed so easily. It was like . . . magic! He reached around Bud for the doorknob.

Thorn's hand shot out and grabbed one of the straps of his backpack.

"Not so fast. You didn't say when we're going to fight. Or where."

"Oh, right." Finch scratched his head. "Cape? What should I tell him?" he asked silently.

You pick a location, Master.

"Well?" With his free hand, Thorn pounded the door above Finch's head.

Finch swallowed. "When it's time for lunch, don't go to the cafeteria. Go outside. The school yard will be empty."

"Good thinking. I guess you don't want to eat first so you won't hurl your lunch." Thorn grinned at his own joke.

"V-very funny!" Finch stammered. "I'll s-see you later."

"Bye-bye, Towelman." Thorn and Bud whooped with laughter as Finch hurried through the door.

"Thanks, Cape," Finch whispered when he was out in the corridor.

My suggestion merely loosened your tongue, Master. It was your words about being discovered by the custodian that stopped them.

Finch felt a little burst of pride. Then reality set in. "What about later? They still want to fight me."

You will need supplies. Bandages, crutches, an ice pack, smelling salts . . .

Finch stopped short. "Hold it! You mean those guys really are going to beat me up? I thought you were supposed to help solve problems."

I am doing my best, Master. But after nearly one thousand years of sleep, I am afraid my powers may be rusty. Besides, it is always better to be safe than sorry.

"Okay." Finch gave up and headed for the nurse's

office. Mrs. Goldstein was dropping pills into a paper cup.

"Hi, Finny, what's wrong?"

"Could I have a Band-Aid?" Finch held up a finger with a tiny cut he'd gotten from his ferrets' cage. "This really stings."

"Sure." Mrs. Goldstein reached into a cabinet.

"Er, could I have a few in case one gets dirty?"

The nurse handed Finch three Band-Aids. When he didn't leave, she crossed her arms over her chest. "Anything else?"

Finch cleared his throat. "Yes. I also need an ice pack, some crutches, and smelling salts."

"What's going on? Are you planning to be injured?"

"No—the opposite. They're to prevent me from getting hurt."

"I don't know, Fin. I think you need to talk to someone about this. A grown-up."

"I already did—a really old, er, advice giver. Please, Mrs. Goldstein, I only need the stuff during lunch recess. I'll bring it back."

The nurse rested her chin in her hand. With one finger, she reached up and tapped her cheek. "Well, okay. I don't know what you're up to, but I'm going to trust you. Stop in on your way to lunch. You'll have to forget about smelling salts, but you can have the crutches and the ice pack as long as you promise to return everything as soon as recess is over."

"I promise. Thanks, Mrs. Goldstein." Finch raced out of the office before she could change her mind.

TO PUNCH OR NOT TO PUNCH

When Finch finally got back to the classroom, he was relieved to see that the guys had arrived. He hurried to their cluster of desks to tell them what had happened.

Raj shook his head. “I can’t believe the cape wants you to fight. It told us it could help solve problems by thinking.”

“Maybe it hasn’t revealed the whole plan yet. It might still have something up its sleeve,” Elliott suggested.

“A cape doesn’t have sleeves,” Kev reminded him.

Finch rubbed his collarbone. The ache he felt was just a taste of what was going to happen to him later—unless some miracle occurred. Because it didn’t look like a thousand-year-old cape with rusty powers was going to be much help.

Suddenly he realized that Ms. Mitchell, the school secretary, was reading the morning announcements over the loudspeaker.

“. . . and Back to School Night is in two weeks. This year, for the first time ever, students are invited to accompany their parents.”

“Yuck,” Kev groaned.

“Yeah—who wants to come to school twice in one day?” Elliott agreed.

“Shh!” Chloe hissed. “I can’t hear.”

“. . . In order to help things run smoothly, we’re looking for a few students to be hospitality captains. It will be their job to help parents and pupils to get around the building, and to see that everyone follows our school rules. If you would like to volunteer, please come to the office.”

Mr. Burns raised his eyebrows. “Anyone want to be a hospitality captain?”

Three hands went up.

"Thorn, you're volunteering?" Mr. Burns sounded doubtful.

"Sure—I'm good at making people follow orders," Thorn said.

Chloe twisted around in her seat. "That's not what Ms. Mitchell meant. You have to be a good host or hostess. I'm experienced. I always help my mother run her Diet Time meetings."

"Ooh! Ooh!" Bud kept waving his hand.

"You want to volunteer too, Bud?" Mr. Burns asked.

Bud nodded. "Do the captains get to wear badges?"

"I don't know." Mr. Burns took a slow, deep breath. "All right—you three may go to Ms. Mitchell's office."

Finch winced. He could just imagine Thorn and Bud ordering the parents around: "Walk, don't run! Spit out that gum! No lingering in the hallways!" With Thorn and Bud as hospitality captains, Back to School Night was going to be more like a Back to School Nightmare. But maybe he wouldn't have to worry about it. He might be dead then, anyway.

When it was time for lunch, he grabbed his backpack and trudged toward the classroom door.

"Hey, dude, is something wrong?" Mr. Burns asked as Finch passed his desk. "You're looking pretty low."

Finch hung his head. He sort of wished he could tell his teacher. But he had his pride—he didn't want to be a tattletale. Besides, Thorn and Bud would just pound him some other time. He wanted to get it over with.

Mr. Burns was waiting for him to answer. Fin racked his brain. "Anthony won't eat. I think maybe he's injured," he blurted out. It was true. When he'd refilled the crabs' food dish, perky Phillip had scuttled right over. But Anthony had just stayed in a corner of the tank.

"It's really nice that you're concerned, Fin. But most hermit crabs eat at night. Anthony's probably been chowing down while you're asleep. Phil is unusual—the little pig will eat anytime."

"Ohhh, right." Finch pressed a hand to his forehead. "I read that on the Web—but I forgot. Thanks."

"Anytime," Mr. Burns said. "You'd better go eat your lunch." He spread a napkin out on his desk and began unzipping his insulated bag as if he were going to eat in the classroom.

"Aren't you going to the teachers' room?" Fin asked before he could stop himself.

"Not today, dude. I want to finish this e-mail to my brother Anthony. I'm inviting him to visit for my birthday."

"When's that?"

"The last day of September."

For a moment, Finch imagined two red-haired bobbleheads nodding at him through the windshield of a car with California license plates. He'd probably been right about Mr. Burns. The guy didn't have any friends here yet.

But right now he had his own problem. Fin raced to the nurse's office. Mrs. Goldstein was busy with a kindergartner who'd lost a tooth, but she had the crutches out for Finch. She told him to take an ice pack out of the fridge.

Finch almost wished he were back in kindergarten. He nudged his backpack with his elbow. "Cape, do you really think this is going to work?" he asked as he pushed through a door that led out to the school yard.

I am a Thinking Cape, not a Promising Cape, Master.

Ugg. Finch felt weak in the knees. But Thorn and Bud were already in the school yard. They were looking at him with joy on their faces.

"We thought maybe you weren't coming," Thorn said. His vampire teeth glinted in the sunlight.

"You brought your own crutches?" Bud squeaked. Finch wondered if he was hopping up and down because he was excited or because he hadn't stopped to use the bathroom. Finch wished he'd used the bathroom himself.

Master, try to get them to move nearer the fence—under the big oak tree.

"Why should I?" Finch said aloud before he realized it.

Thorn squinted an eye at him. "Who are you talking to?"

"No one! I mean, we'd better move away from school, in case someone's looking out the window. Maybe that tree will block the view."

Bud scowled. "He's stalling. There's not much time before everyone gets out of the cafeteria."

Thorn shrugged. "Don't worry. It will only take a few seconds to make him cry like a baby."

Finch felt a trickle of sweat run down his back as he led Thorn and Bud to the oak tree.

"Okay, Towelman. Drop your backpack and get ready." Thorn already had his fists up.

"Wait! Just let me get out the rest of my supplies." Finch fell to his knees and began taking out the Band-Aids, the ice pack, and a water bottle. He crouched down and arranged them on the grass next to the crutches. Maybe Bud had been right about stalling. Maybe that was the Thinking Cape's plan.

"Haw, haw, haw! You brought your own hospital," Thorn cracked. "Good idea!"

Master! Tell him the supplies are not for you.

Finch was confused. But there was no time to ask questions. "These first-aid supplies aren't for me," he said. He pulled some tissues out of his pocket and added them to the display in case someone ended up with a bloody nose or was crying.

Thorn smirked. "Oh yeah? Then who are they for?"

Suddenly Finch understood what the cape was up to. He stared Thorn in the eyes. "They're for you."

As if those three words were a cue, Raj, Elliott, and Kev stepped out from behind the tree.

"Hey, what is this—an ambush?" Thorn demanded.

"No fair," Bud whined.

"Guys! What are you doing here?" Finch exclaimed. He was as surprised as Thorn and Bud.

"We're your cheering section," Elliott announced.

"Yeah, we're here for moral support," Raj said. But Finch noticed he'd removed his glasses as if he were expecting to be in a fight.

Kevin stuck out his bulldog chest. "For your information, Fin doesn't need our help. So you'd better hurry up and start fighting. That ice pack's melting and you're going to need it afterward."

Thorn gnashed his teeth. He stabbed a finger into Fin's skinny biceps. "They're lying! If you can fight, why didn't you stop me from spraying soda all over you?"

Finch hesitated. His arm hurt.

Master! Remember the gift or the curse.

"When people find out you've got a gift, they're always bothering you to use it," Finch said. "You know, like Spider-Man."

Thorn narrowed his eyes. "Huh?"

"I figured if it got out I could fight, kids would be challenging me all the time. Just because I can fight doesn't mean I like to hurt people. I've got self-control."

"That's bull!"

"Okay, then forget it." Finch stuck out his chin. "Go on and hit me."

Nay, Master, nay! I fear you are crossing the line from bravery to foolishness.

Thorn made a fist and pulled back his arm.

Finch stood his ground. He locked eyes with Thorn. He tried his best to look unafraid.

"You think you're so smart, don't you, Towelman? Well, if you're not going to use your gift, I'm not going to use mine either. I've got self-control, too." Thorn let his arm drop.

For a moment, no one seemed to know what to do next. Then the school doors opened and students began pouring out into the yard.

"Come on." Thorn gave Bud a shove. "Let's get out of here."

Silently, the members of the SSSh watched Thorn and Bud cross the field. All at once, they turned to one another and began shouting.

"Ye-es!"

"You did it, Fin!"

"Thorny actually looked scared."

"It was the Thinking Cape's idea." Finch nodded toward his backpack. "Thanks, Cape," he whispered.

You are welcome, Master Finch. But I am afraid it is too early to celebrate.

"Why?"

A melon seed in the ground may one day reappear a thousand times bigger and fatter and pop you in the nose.

THE MISSION

"We've got exactly seventy-two minutes," Raj whispered as he closed the door to his room. He'd just put his "secret weapon," a DVD of *The Jungle Book,* into the DVD player. It was the best way to keep his twin siblings, Sonny and Meena, in the living room.

While the guys spread out on Raj's red rug, Fin draped the Thinking Cape over his back. On the bus, he'd told the guys he had an idea for their first official mission. But he wasn't sure how to begin. He knew his friends were expecting something adventurous or even risky—especially after his showdown with Thorn and Bud. But his idea wasn't either of those things.

Elliott rubbed his hands together. "Come on! What's the mission already?"

"It's not a 'what' exactly, it's more of a 'who,'" Finch said carefully. "It's Mr. Burns. He had lunch alone in the classroom today. He never hangs out in the hall with the other teachers. And he told me he invited his brother in California to come for his birthday at the end of the month. I bet he hasn't got any friends here. I think we should help him make some."

Kevin snorted. "That's not a superheroes' mission!"

"Yes, it is. We're supposed to do our best to help others. We're supposed to solve problems," Finch reminded him. "Being lonely is a problem. Having no friends is a problem."

Kev crossed his arms over his chest. "It's the most boring thing I ever heard. Superhero missions are supposed to be exciting."

"Yeah, but we're still beginners," Raj pointed out. "We can pick tougher ones later on when we're ready."

"What about Miss Pesco, the new kindergarten

teacher?" Elliott suggested. "She might need a friend. Maybe we could get her and Mr. Burns together."

"A girl?" Kev scoffed.

"So what?" Elliott was the only one of the superheroes who had friend-girls in school. "Girls have some good points. They don't finish their snacks, so you get to eat their leftovers. They laugh at your worst jokes. You can gross them out easily. And they always have an extra pencil you can borrow."

"I don't really think you can pick a friend for someone else," Fin said thoughtfully. "I think our mission should be to help Mr. Burns meet a lot of people. That way he can find the right one himself."

"How are we going to do that?" Elliott asked.

Finch shrugged. "I'm not sure."

May I suggest a birthday party, Master?

"Yeah! What about a surprise party?" El exclaimed.

"Who would we invite?" Raj asked.

Fin ran his fingers through the shaggy rug. He was trying not to seem too excited. "We could invite the other teachers. And the principal, and Ms. Mitchell, and all the other adults that work at school."

"I don't want to go to a party with only grown-ups," Kev objected.

"We'd invite our classmates, too," Fin told him.

Raj nodded. "It might work."

"Raji! Raji!" Suddenly the four-year-olds, Meena and Sonny, came bursting through the door.

"The DVD stopped!" Meena announced.

"I think it's broken," Sonny wailed.

"Oh, man!" Raj put his arms around the twins. "Let's go back to the living room and I'll see if I can fix it." He tried to guide them out of his room.

But Sonny was staring at the cape. "What's that?" Before anyone realized what was happening, he grabbed it.

"It's Fin's, Sonny," Raj said. "Give it back."

But Sonny held the cape out with both hands and stared at the bright yellow lightning bolts. "Can I have it, Fin? Pleeease?"

Finch had to force himself not to grab it away. But he only said, "No, Sonny. I'm sorry."

Raj held out his hand. "C'mon. Give it to me."

"But I want it!" Sonny hugged the cape tightly to his little chest and glared at Finch. "Big boys don't wear these!"

Raj pushed his glasses up on his nose. "We can ask Naani to make you one. I think we have an old green towel in the basement." Naani was their grandmother. Right now she was in the kitchen cooking dinner.

"I want this one!" Sonny burst into tears. Meena had been standing by quietly. But when she saw her twin crying, she began weeping, too.

"Shh! Shh! How about if I show you a magic trick?" Raj pulled a white handkerchief from a drawer in his desk. "I'll make the little ghost appear."

Meena's cries softened into sniffles. But Sonny

shook his head fiercely. “No!” he screamed. Tears and snot were running down his face. He wiped them on the cape.

Feh! Feh! Pfu! Pfu!

“Sonny, it’s just a crummy old towel. Give it to me now,” Raj ordered as he grabbed hold of the cape.

Sonny kicked him.

“Ow! Ow!” Raj rubbed his leg. “No hurting!”

Sonny lay down on the floor. He rolled himself up in the cape. “Miiine!” he wailed.

The guys all looked at one another.

“You two take his head,” Raj told El and Kev. “Fin and I will take his feet.” Together, the guys lifted Sonny off the floor. They set him on the bed and began to unroll him. Sonny twisted, squirmed, and cried. He bit down on the cape.

Aiyyyaaa!!!

“Let go, Sonny,” Finch said. “You’ll tear my cape.”

“Rrrrrrr,” Sonny growled through his teeth.

Finch leaned over and whispered to Elliott. “Do you have your rubber snot with you? Maybe he’ll trade it for it.”

“Forget it! It comes from England! It cost five bucks plus seven more for shipping and handling.”

"Come on, El, it isn't magic snot. You can get another one. I'll help you pay for it," Finch pleaded.

"Oookaaay." El stuck his hand into his pocket. "But how come if the Thinking Cape is so smart, it can't save itself?"

SUPER-TRADE

Stomach churning, Finch hurried home with the Thinking Cape around his shoulders. It had asked to feel fresh air and sunshine. How could he refuse—it had practically saved his life today! If he ran into any of the neighbors, he planned to say it was his costume for a play at school.

"Cape, I've been wondering about something. Didn't I hear your voice in my head before I guessed your name?"

Yes, Master.

"But isn't it against the rules? You said you're only supposed to speak to those who know you're a Thinking Cape."

Yes, Master, it is true. Since the day you found me, I hoped you would be the one to uncover my identity. It seemed that you were getting close when you suddenly decided to toss me away. So I gave you a little help in order to change your mind.

"You broke the rules?"

Not broke, Master—bent. I never spoke the words Thinking Cape *in your head. You puzzled them out on your own.*

"It was just luck," Fin said. They were in front of his house now. He pressed the doorbell. Then he thought of one more question. "What happened to all the other capes from your cape maker's shop? Do you know where they are now?"

Nay, Master. I think perchance I am alone in the world.

Finch reached up and stroked his shoulder. He'd never thought about the cape being lonely. "Maybe they're just in hiding—like you," he whispered.

Suddenly the door flew open. "What do you want?" Mimi snapped. She'd tied a red bandanna over her hair, and she was wearing an old T-shirt with nail-polish stains. She looked more like Gloria, the cleaning lady, than her usual supermodelish self.

"Doh—I live here." Finch pushed past her into the house and stomped toward his room. But a mountain of junk in the hallway stopped him. Rosie and Cubby were climbing over it as if it were some new kind of ferret jungle gym.

"What's this stuff doing here?" he asked as he picked up a pair of old shin guards.

"I'm having a yard sale to raise money for the tuition to private school." Mimi was right behind him.

"But these are mine."

"So? They're too small for you, anyway. You haven't worn them since first grade."

"You can't have them!" Finch hugged the plastic shields to his chest. "I'm saving them for when Jake gets bigger."

"Uh-huh." Mimi pursed her lips in the same unconvinced look his mother sometimes gave him.

He ignored her and eyed the rest of the stuff she'd collected. Piles of paperbacks; old figure skates (Rosie now had her head in one); a little pink backpack; a Barbie bus (Cubby was climbing into it); a Betty

Crocker Easy-Bake Oven that Finch had once secretly yearned for himself; his stuffed tiger, Daniel; and—

"Hey!" he yelped. "You can't sell Daniel."

"Why not? You don't play with it anymore. We should definitely sell this, too. I can't believe you're actually wearing it." Mimi plucked the cape off Fin's shoulders and tossed it onto the pile.

O sister with tongue of vicious venom!

"Give that back!" Finch yanked the cape off a rickety old ferret cage. It was the one the pet store had given them free for buying two baby ferrets. Since then, they'd bought Rosie and Cubby a super-deluxe ferret condo.

"I thought you were through with superheroes."

"I am. But this cape is my . . . my . . . history!" Finch sputtered.

Mimi fingered the satin strings thoughtfully. "I remember when you brought this thing home from the garage sale. For a secondhand towel, it's in amazingly good shape. It doesn't look worn out at all."

Finch shrugged. "Maybe it's because it doesn't get washed very often."

Mimi sniffed the cape. "It doesn't even stink. I bet I could get two dollars for it."

Two dollars? My first master paid five chests of gold for me.

"Well, you can't have it—or any of my stuff." Finch tugged the strings out of her hand. He took a good look at the pile again. "You're selling your shell collection?"

Mimi eyed the box of shells scornfully. "I got most of them with Kelly two years ago when her parents took us to Cape Cod. I don't want them anymore."

"Can I have them?" Finch was already reaching for the box.

"Nope—not unless you let me have your junk to sell."

"All right. I guess you can have these." Finch held out the shin guards.

"What about the rest?"

"What? The shin guards are worth more than those shells."

"Not to me." Mimi started to walk away. "I'm going to check the spare room for more stuff."

Finch took a deep breath. "Okay. I'll let you have Daniel. Just don't sell him to anyone with little kids that look like biters or kickers." He gave the scraggly tiger a farewell pat.

Mimi tossed Daniel back on her pile. "What about the cape?"

"I'M NOT GIVING YOU MY CAPE!" Finch screamed.

O valorous Master who fends off the she-tiger!

Mimi's mouth settled into a smirk. "You don't have to be a baby about it. Keep your stupid cape. I'll let you have the shells—if you help me drag this stuff over to the garage. There's so much to do to be ready by next Saturday. I've got to make signs to hang around the neighborhood, and put price tags on everything. And I'm going to make cookies and lemonade to sell."

Finch wished he could put a price tag on his sister and sell her. But he picked up a stack of books and followed her into the garage.

"Does Mom know you want to go to private school?"

"Yes."

"So she's for it?"

"Not exactly. She thinks I'm just having a hard time adjusting to seventh grade. She says I should be patient. She's sure Kelly and I will make up." Mimi rolled her eyes back so far, they were hidden under her bangs.

"Maybe Mom's right." Finch set down the stack of books.

"No way. Kelly doesn't care about me. Holly is her new best friend now."

"That really stinks," Finch said in a froggy voice. If the guys decided not to be friends with him anymore, he wouldn't want to go to school either. One day last year, Raj, Kev, and Elliott had all been absent. Finch hadn't had anyone to sit with at lunch. He still remembered how uncomfortable he'd felt.

Mimi nodded. "Mom says if I can make half the money for private school, she and Dad will pay the rest."

"How much is that?"

"I think about seven thousand dollars."

Finch's jaw dropped. "Mimi, you can't make that kind of money selling junk and cleaning the house!"

"Yes, I can. I have to! Otherwise, I'll move in with Dad and Lisa and go to school in their district." Mimi marched back into the house for more stuff.

Finch ran after her. "Look, Dad doesn't want us now that he's got Jake. The blob is all he thinks about."

"Maybe he doesn't want you, but I could be a lot

of help. I know how to change a diaper. I could babysit."

Finch had to swallow back a lump in his throat. There were lots of times he wished he didn't have a sister. But that was because he'd never thought it could happen. Besides, he'd never let the blob have her—he already had their dad.

Fin picked up the old ferret cage. "What if Kelly wanted to be your friend again?"

"Forget it. It's not going to happen."

"You never know. Something could change her mind."

"I'm still having the sale, Fin."

"But you'd like it, right?"

Mimi's chin trembled. "I guess so."

"Cape?" Finch asked silently. "Would you help me fix things up between Mimi and Kelly?"

I am a Thinking Cape, not a miracle worker, Master.

"But you're supposed to help solve problems. You haven't even tried."

"Perchance later, after a nap. I am feeling tired now. Besides, a little suffering may help to sweeten up that sour she-fruit. Would you not like that?"

"No!"

"No what?" Mimi asked over her shoulder.

"Nothing," Finch answered quickly. He'd forgotten to speak in his head. He pressed his lips tightly together to keep it from happening again. "I don't want Mimi to suffer," he said in his mind. "I thought you were supposed to obey me."

But, Master, when the fruit is already spoiled, it is too late to make a jam with it.

"Pell-mell, a speechless spell!" Finch chanted silently. Then he carried the cage to the garage.

Finch waited until the lights were out in his mother's and sister's rooms before he sneaked into the spare room where they kept the computer. He closed the door and switched the desk lamp on low. He even remembered to turn down the sound as the computer booted up. He was hoping to find information on the Internet about Thinking Capes. If his cape had survived all this time, there might be others, too. It would be especially great if he could find one owned by another kid. Then they could e-mail about questions or problems.

At first he Googled "Thinking Capes." But he only found a site called Planet of the Capes, and one about women's fashions in Victorian England. He tried "Magic Capes" next, but that brought up a lot of online costume shops. He was beginning to feel discouraged when he remembered the cape mentioning that it was from a town near Persia or Arabia, so he typed in "Persia," "Arabia," and "Magic Capes." Up came Magic Carpet Tours (but that was only a travel agency) and a lot of places that sold Oriental rugs.

Enough! He was about to shut down the computer when his eye fell on a line at the bottom of the screen: Tales from the Arabian Nights . . . tales of magic and mystery. He clicked on it.

A book called *Tales from the Arabian Nights* appeared on the screen. The cover had a genie with muscles like the Incredible Hulk rising up from a thing that looked like a golden pitcher. Finch knew from the animated movie he'd seen that it was supposed to be Aladdin's lamp. But this seemed quite realistic, not like the cartoon kind. The line Search inside this book appeared on the screen. Finch clicked.

The first page was an introduction. It said the tales in the book first began appearing over a thousand years ago in places like India, Persia, and Arabia. Finch felt a buzz of recognition. He looked at the table of contents. None of the titles had the words *magic cape* in them, but they did have other enchanted items, like keys of destiny and everlasting shoes. Maybe there would be clues about other magical capes in those stories. Tomorrow, he'd stop in the school library and see if he could find the book.

He got back to his room without waking anyone. The Thinking Cape was in a corner of his bed, exactly where he'd left it. "Hi, Cape," he whispered.

The cape was silent.

Finch reached out and shook it. The cape still didn't answer. Then he remembered about the spell.

"Quell, quell the speechless spell!" he chanted.

Hello, Master. How may I help you?

"Just saying good night," Fin said with a yawn.

Master? I would sleep better if I could feel the night breeze. Would you mind opening the window before you go to sleep?

"Sure." Finch pushed up the window. A soft breeze stirred the curtains. He lay down and fell into a deep, refreshing sleep.

YARD SALE TODAY

Under the shade of a red maple tree, Finch was manning his sister's lemonade and cookie stand. His backpack hung from a branch overhead, top open so the Thinking Cape could get the fresh air it craved. It swung lightly in the breeze, although occasionally an early fall gust sent it twisting wildly. Rosie and Cubby were getting some fresh air as well. Fin had covered a few sharp wires on their old cage with tape and set it in the grass nearby. The ferrets climbed up and down, poking their little noses through the bars.

They were so excited to be out-of-doors, they were squeaking.

Fin filled six paper cups with lemonade and set them out on the table. He rearranged the chocolate chip cookies more neatly on the tray. Then he helped himself to one and plopped down in a lawn chair.

All over the front yard, strangers were picking

through his family's unwanted stuff. His mother had decided a yard sale was a good opportunity to clean out the house.

While he waited for lemonade customers, he opened the copy of *Tales from the Arabian Nights* he'd found at the school library. Last night he'd read one of the stories to the Thinking Cape—"Sinbad the Sailor and the Valley of Diamonds." It was awesome! Dangling from the claw of an enormous bird, Sinbad had flown into a valley that sparkled with emeralds, diamonds, and rubies. But when the bird landed, Sinbad discovered the floor of the valley was also covered with snakes so big they could swallow a man as easily as you could swallow your chewing gum. Before Sinbad realized what was happening, the humongous bird sucked up one of the snakes like a worm and flew off. Now Sinbad was trapped—the sides of the valley were as straight as walls and as slick as glass. No human had ever climbed out.

But Sinbad the Sailor never gave up. He stuck some of the jewels in his pockets for later and hid under the old, smelly carcass of a donkey that must have fallen off the cliff. After a long wait, the giant bird came along again. This time it plucked up the rotten carcass (with Sinbad hanging on beneath) and flew back to its nest to feed the meat to its chicks. While the birds were busy, Sinbad escaped before he became bird food, too.

"Pee-yew, Sinbad must have really smelled when he got out of there," Finch had commented when he'd finished reading. "But he sure was smart. I think he should have been called Sinbad the Thinking Sailor."

The cape had huffed in disagreement.

That sailor was not so clever. I, too, visited that valley with my old master, the merchant.

"What!" Finch exclaimed before he could stop himself. He looked around. Fortunately, no one had heard him. He pressed his palm over his mouth and continued inside his head, "You went down into that valley? With all those snakes?"

Nay, Master, there was no need. I knew that serpents enjoyed eating warty toads much more than munching men. So I had the merchant bring two sacks. One was filled with fat, croaking creatures. The other was empty. Off we rode to the edge of the cliff above the valley. When my master looked down and saw the writhing, hissing snakes, he nearly fainted. But I advised him to toss a few of the toads over the edge. As he did so, the serpents' appetites were greatly aroused. "Moooore!" they hissed.

"Now it is time to bargain," I told my master. "Toss the empty sack down into the valley and have the serpents fill it with jewels. Tell them if they bring it up here, you will give them a sack full of toads."

My master was afraid the sinister serpents would eat the toads and the two of us as well. But I told him not to worry, for I had a plan. As soon as the awful creatures brought up the sack of jewels, I had the merchant toss the bag of toads over the edge of the cliff. Quickly, the serpents slithered back down to catch them. That is how, without risking his life, my master came away richer than a king.

Finch thought for a moment. "But the stories in this book are made up. They aren't true."

Most stories begin with real experience, Master. I hope you do not think I am a teller of untruths?

"No, of course not," Finch answered quickly. "You were really smart—and brave."

Thank you, Master.

"You're welcome." Fin chewed his last bite of cookie thoughtfully. "If the sides of the valley were like glass walls, how did the snakes climb them?"

They had suction cups on their undersides, Master, like the arms of an octopus.

"Then why did they stay in the valley? Why didn't they crawl up and find their own toads?"

Really, Master Finch, it is quite simple. They were too lazy.

"Oh," Finch said, although it didn't seem so simple to him. But it hadn't sounded as if the Thinking Cape wanted to answer any more questions.

A sudden burst of wind sent his stack of paper napkins flying. He ran around the table to retrieve them.

"Hi, Finny."

Finch looked up into the face of his sister's ex–best friend, Kelly Clark. She was with a girl he didn't recognize—and two guys he did.

"This is Holly," Kelly said. Her cheeks had more freckles than he remembered. It felt like a long time since he'd seen her, although really, it had only been a few weeks.

Finch slid his eyes over to the other girl. She had short black hair, big blue eyes, and a mouth that hung open as if she were bored. This girl was the reason his sister and Kelly weren't best friends anymore. He narrowed his eyes at her.

"And these two guys are Ollie Rosebud and his brother—" Kelly continued.

"I know, I know," Finch snapped. He glared at Bud.

Kelly rolled her bottom lip into a pout. "Aren't you going to say hello?"

Finch peered across the lawn to where his sister was showing someone a lamp. He looked back at Kelly and shrugged.

"We'll have four lemonades," Ollie Rosebud said.

Finch squinted up at him. Ollie had a deep voice and biceps you could actually see. He smelled as if he wore underarm deodorant. Probably the girls thought he was hot.

Finch slid four cups across the table. "That will be three dollars."

"They're supposed to be fifty cents a cup."

With a black marker, Finch changed the sign from fifty cents to seventy-five. "The price just went up."

Ollie scowled. "Forget it. Let's look around." He grabbed Bud by the back of the neck and hauled him away. Holly went with them, but Kelly lingered behind.

"Come on, Kel," Holly called.

"I'll be there in a minute. I want to say hello to the ferrets."

Holly stuck out her tongue. "Ew, they look like giant rats."

"No, they don't." Kelly knelt in front of the cage. "Hi, Rosie. Hi, Cubby," she crooned. "I've missed you."

Finch had a hunch she missed his sister, too. If Kelly didn't want to be friends with Mimi again, why would she have come today? He looked up at his backpack and sent an urgent message: "Cape, wake up! Mimi's ex-friend Kelly is here. Did you think of a way to get them back together yet?"

Master, be reasonable. The powers of a Thinking Cape are limited to what is possible. Who can make peace between a she-lion and a she-tiger?

Finch glanced over at his sister. She was staring at Kelly. But when Kelly looked back, Mimi turned away. "My sister isn't a wild beast," he told the cape. "She's only a girl—a very unhappy one. If you really figured out how to take diamonds away from snakes, you should be able to solve a little problem like this."

In a few moments, the wind picked up. It blew across the lawn and swept the tables. Toys, knickknacks, paperbacks, and other items flew off onto the grass.

"Help!" Mimi called as the wind got stronger. She tried to keep the tables from overturning.

Finch hurried toward her, snatching things up on his way.

"Finny, wait! The ferrets!" Kelly yelled.

Finch whirled around. He saw the door to the old ferret cage swinging back and forth in the wind. Rosie and Cubby were scampering across the yard. "Mimi! Rosie and Cubby are out," he shouted as he began chasing them.

The ferrets disappeared among the shoppers and the items scattered on the lawn.

"Rosie, Cubby!" Mimi got down on her hands and knees to peer under a table.

"Rosie, Cubby!" Kelly poked in the bushes at the side of the house.

"Rosie, Cubby, where are you?" Finch scanned the trees. He looked under cars parked in front of the house. Suddenly, from behind a tire, he saw a cinnamon-colored tail twitch. He reached under the car and scooped up the ferret.

"Ew, ew, ew!" a voice shrieked. "Help!"

Finch spun around. Holly was bent over at the waist. Her hands were covering her face. Poor, frightened Rosie had climbed up onto her back and was hiding in the hood of her sweatshirt jacket.

Running from different directions, Mimi and Kelly reached her at the same time.

"Ooh, ooh, get it off! Get the rat off of me!" Holly shrieked. Nearby, Ollie and Bud were laughing hysterically.

"Be quiet, you're frightening her," Mimi ordered as she lifted Rosie out of the hood. She glared at Ollie and Bud. "And you losers shut up, too."

Finch couldn't help grinning.

"I already told you not to call her a rat. She's a ferret," Kelly told Holly. "She's the sweetest, most gentle creature in the world."

"Sorry," Holly said. "I never saw one of those before."

"I'd better bring them both inside in case the wind starts gusting again," Finch offered.

"Here." Mimi tucked Rosie into the crook of his other arm.

Kelly put a hand lightly on Mimi's shoulder. "I'll help you fix up the tables—if that's okay."

"Sure." Mimi flashed a mile-wide grin. They began walking off together, shoulders touching. Then Mimi stopped and turned. "Come on, Holly, you can help, too."

Finch was pretty sure his sister was going to have two best friends soon. He headed for the house with Rosie and Cubby. When he was far enough away, he checked to see that no one was watching him. Then he gave each of the ferrets a quick kiss on their furry heads.

Master Finch, help!

Fin was just coming outside again when the cape's voice filled his head. He gazed at the tree branch. His backpack was gone. He scanned the lawn and spotted it lying there. But when he picked it up and looked inside, it was empty.

Please hurry, O valorous lion! I am about to be sold.

Finch looked around until he saw a flutter of green. A boy of about four or five was wearing the Thinking Cape. It dragged behind him on the ground as he ran across the yard. For a second, Finch felt as if he were looking at his old self.

"Eric, don't run with that on or you'll trip, honey," a woman called. "I'll cut it down when we get home." She held some bills out to Mimi.

Aiyyya! Scissors will snip away my power!

"Wait!" Finch shouted as he bolted to the table. "That cape is mine."

Everyone on the lawn turned to look at him.

"It was on the table," the woman said. "That means it's for sale." She waved her bills.

"It wasn't supposed to be here. It blew out of my backpack," Finch said more quietly. His ears began burning. He felt like a jerk.

The woman eyed him up and down. "My little boy really likes it. Surely a big guy like you can understand."

Finch rubbed his eye with a fist. "But my grandma made it for me, and she's not . . . um . . . she's not here anymore."

For a moment, Mimi gave him a wide-eyed look. Then she put her arm around him. "I'm really sorry, but we can't sell it," she said sweetly. "My brother and my grandmother were very close. The cape is like an heirloom to him."

"Oh, I see." The woman put her money away. "You should have said so." She gave Finch a sympathetic pat on the shoulder.

"Here—give your son this. It's free." Finch held out Daniel, his old tiger.

"That's very nice of you." The woman carried the stuffed animal over to her boy. Finch followed behind her.

"Look at this, Eric." As the kid examined the tiger, his mother untied the cape strings. "I'm sorry about your grandmother," she told Fin as she handed him the cape.

"Er, thanks," Finch said uncomfortably. His grandma lived in Miami Beach, Florida. She could swim more laps in her condo's pool than he could.

"Cape—did you stir up the wind?" he asked silently as he carried it across the lawn.

I do not know for certain, though I might have, Master.

"You might have? You never told me you could do anything but think."

While I sat on a shelf waiting to be purchased, I could not help hearing the weavers whisper many types of magic spells. I may have remembered one.

"Do you remember any others?"

Nay, Master. After more than a thousand years, the words are lost to me. But perchance over time they will return.

Finch stroked the cape as if it were one of the ferrets. "Thanks for helping my sister the she-tiger."

It is I who owe you thanks, Master Finch. Your quick thinking kept me from being sold. Who knows what would have become of me?

"That little kid didn't look so bad. But I'd better put you away now before someone else tries to buy you."

Yes, Master. I had no idea how dangerous a yard sale could be.

That gave Finch a chuckle. The cape had faced a valley full of man-eating snakes, yet it thought a yard sale was dangerous. He shook his head as he tucked it into his backpack. "You're too much, Cape!" he said aloud.

When he looked up, he saw Bud staring at him.

SHELL SHOCK

"Wake up, Anthony. It's Monday morning. Look what I've got for you." Finch lifted the screen and lowered a swirly white shell into the tank. The minute he'd spotted it in his sister's collection, he knew it would be perfect for the little crab. Carefully, he set it in on the bottom. For a change Anthony didn't hide. On the ends of their stalks, his eyes watched the new object.

"Go for it!" Finch whispered. "It's nice and roomy—it will make you look like a big shot."

For a moment, Anthony's two longer antennae seemed to reach toward the new shell. But they stopped short of actually touching it.

"Aw, come on." Finch was so frustrated he flicked a finger against the tank. That sent Anthony withdrawing into his old shell.

"Oops, sorry," Finch apologized. On the Internet he'd seen pictures of hermit crabs without their shells. Their pale, hairless bellies had made him think of raw chicken. Yech. Probably Anthony would change his shell at night when he had more privacy. That's what Finch would do if he were a hermit crab.

"I'll check on you later, boy," he whispered. He looked around for something to do. Last night he'd finished all his homework and read the end of the third book in *A Series of Unfortunate Events*. As usual, Mr. Burns was on the computer.

Finch cleared his throat. "Mr. Burns?"

"Yes?" his teacher answered without looking up.

"Do you want to show me any new yoga positions? I'm pretty good at the scorpion now."

"Sure. Just let me finish this e-mail to my brother."

"Is he going to come here for your birthday?"

"Nope." Mr. Burns shrugged a shoulder. "We've

decided to wait until winter break and go skiing together."

"Oh." Even though Mr. Burns didn't sound upset, Finch felt bad for him. Last winter, for the first time, his father hadn't been at his birthday dinner. The blob had just been born, and Lisa wasn't feeling well enough to be left alone. So Fin had gone out for pizza with his mom and Mimi. Although he'd eaten four slices, he'd still left with a strange, empty feeling.

Suddenly Mr. Burns clapped him on the back. "How's your balance?"

"Okay, I guess."

"Good. Come on, I'll show you the eagle."

Later, Mr. Burns was reading *The Indian in the Cupboard* aloud when the noise started up. *Chhhhirup, chhhhirup, chhhhirup!*

"I think there's a frog in the classroom," someone called out.

"It sounds more like a chicken," another person said.

"It's just a cricket," Chloe announced, as sure of herself as ever.

Mr. Burns frowned. "That's the noise of a hermit-crab fight."

The crabs! Finch jumped up and ran to the tank. Anthony's old shell was lying on its side. Finch could see it was empty. The little crab must have moved into the new shell. But it looked like Phillip wanted it, too. With his walking claws, the bigger crab was shaking the swirly shell back and forth. His big claw poked into the opening as if he were trying to pinch Anthony.

"Phillip, stop—leave Anthony alone!" Finch yelped.

The entire class scrambled to the Critter Corner to watch.

Finch lifted the cover off the tank and reached inside. He tried to pull the crabs apart. Suddenly Phillip pinched the web of skin between his thumb and forefinger.

"Ouch!" Finch shook his hand free. Phillip went back to poking at Anthony. The chirping in the tank got louder and faster.

Finch grabbed the misting bottle and began pumping so fast he created a rainstorm in the tank. To his relief, Phillip released Anthony and began backing away from the spray. Fin's classmates cheered. But in another moment, Anthony's grayish-white body slid out of the new shell.

"Look, it's sushi!" Thorn yelled.

Some of the kids laughed. But Finch was horrified. Was Anthony dead? He wasn't moving at all.

Suddenly Thorn shouted, "Crab attack! Crab attack!"

Bud pumped his fist. "Phillip's gonna eat the sushi."

Zoe, Chloe, and Kayla started squealing as Phillip scuttled toward Anthony again. His fighting claw was up and ready. But he just climbed over Anthony and kept going. Then he slipped out of his old shell and flipped his saggy abdomen into the swirly new one.

"Ooooh." The kids breathed as if they were one giant organism.

"No fair! He stole Anthony's home," Elliott complained.

Still and limp, Anthony lay on the gravel. He didn't look as if he would be needing a home anymore.

"I thought a bigger shell would help," Finch croaked. "I thought it would make Anthony feel proud so he wouldn't be so shy or scared. I never thought Phillip would—" The rest of the words got choked in his throat.

"I want everyone back in their seats," Mr. Burns ordered in a quiet voice. "Anthony is very stressed out right now. We need to leave him alone and hope that he recovers. No running or jumping near his tank. No loud noises. He may move back into his or Phillip's old shell."

Thorn raised his hand. "What if he doesn't? 'Cause I read that a healthy crab will sometimes eat a dying one." He twisted around and smirked at Finch.

O son of a scorpion! May you sit upon your own stinger!

The Thinking Cape's words were like rocket fuel in Fin's veins. They launched him up out of his chair. "SHUT UP, YOU SCORPION! I HOPE YOU SIT ON YOUR STINGER!" he screamed at Thorn. Without waiting for Mr. Burns to say anything, he grabbed his backpack and sent himself to the principal's office. As he ran down the corridor, he could hear his class-mates laughing.

INVITING TROUBLE

When the students came in after recess, Finch was back at his desk. He was reading one of Mr. Burns's books about hermit crabs.

"What happened?" Raj whispered as he slipped into the chair beside him. "What did Mr. Kutler say?"

"He said since I already knew I shouldn't have disrupted the class, I didn't need a lecture. But he made me stay for a cooling-off period. I helped him organize his books and magazines, and he got us pizza for lunch. Afterward, he told me to go and apologize to Mr. Burns."

Elliott's mouth opened so wide, a pigeon could have flown inside. "I can't believe you had pizza with the principal! Tomorrow I'm going to tell someone in class to shut up."

"What about Mr. Burns? Was he mad?" Kev asked.

"Not exactly. He used the word *disappointed.* He said he didn't know what had come over me." Finch shook his head. Actually, he knew what had made him lose it—the Thinking Cape. It had been what his mom would call "a bad influence."

Kev scowled. "Mr. Burns should have sent Thorn to the principal's office."

"Yeah. But it wasn't so bad," Finch said. "I got to see Anthony move back into his old shell. It happened when I got back to the room. Mr. Burns watched with me."

"At least Anthony is okay," Raj said.

Finch glanced at the tank. "For now."

"I know one person who's still really mad." Kevin jerked his head toward Thorn. "At recess, Tyler and Pierre started calling him Thorpion. You should've seen how mad he looked—like he was going to bite their heads off. It's a good thing my mom is picking us up today. At least you won't run into him on the way home." The guys were going to Kev's house to make invitations for Mr. Burns's birthday party.

Finch let out a sigh. Now he knew what the cape had meant when it said, *A melon seed in the ground may one day reappear a thousand times bigger and fatter and pop you in the nose*. Trouble was coming. Maybe he'd get to avoid it today. But just like the Thinking Cape, he could sense that it was on its way.

Kev's mom was waiting in her minivan when the guys got out of school. "How was your day, boys?" she asked as they buckled themselves in.

Everyone but Finch answered, "Fine." The word that described his day couldn't be said in front of Mrs. Chan.

Kev fished out a pack of markers from the seat pocket in front of him. He had markers stashed all over—under his pillow, in the bottom of his sleeping bag, and in the toothbrush holder in his bathroom. He pulled out a pad. "Does anyone have an idea for the cover of the invitations?"

"We could draw balloons," Raj suggested.

"B-O-R-I-N-G," Elliott spelled.

Kev began doodling. "What about a bugle? Only

instead of *Flaaah,* it could have the word *Shhh* coming out of the bottom." He turned his paper around so the guys could see. In just a few strokes, he'd drawn a bugle with a curving tube, a bell-shaped bottom, and three buttons on top.

"That's awesome," Elliott said.

"Yeah," Finch agreed. The sketch looked so real he could almost hear it go *Flaaah!*

"What are you guys making back there?" Mrs. Chan asked.

"A card for our teacher's birthday," Kev answered. It was mostly true. An invitation was a type of card.

"We'd better get busy right away," Raj said softly. "We need to make enough cards for all the teachers, the other school staff, and our classmates."

"Except Thorn and Bud," Fin whispered.

Raj blinked at him. "We've got to invite them. We can't just leave them out."

"Why not?" Fin hissed. He felt like shouting, but he didn't want Mrs. Chan to hear.

"Because they'll kill us when they find out about it," Elliott murmured.

"Forget it," Fin mouthed. He leaned back against the seat and shut his eyes until Kev's mother pulled into the driveway.

The boys dashed into Kev's room and spread out around his worktable. Kev dropped a briefcase full of markers and a stack of paper in the middle.

"We're not inviting Thorn and Bud," Finch insisted while he tied on the Thinking Cape.

Perchance you should reconsider, Master. That does not seem like a wise idea.

Finch shrugged a shoulder. "No one asked you. You're a thinking cape, not a manners cape."

But, Master Finch, this party is for Mr. Burns. He would not want to hurt the feelings of any of his students. Not even if one is a scorpion and the other a dung beetle.

"Dung beetle?" Raj exclaimed. "My grandma told me they've got those in India—giant ones that eat elephant poop."

"Elephant poop!" Elliott and Kev began screaming with laughter. But Finch felt a flicker of irritation.

"I'm the master around here, not you," he snapped at the cape. "Quit telling me what to do."

I am sorry, Master. I was only trying to be helpful.

Kev was still cackling. "I think the cape is right, *Master*. It's Mr. Burns's party, not yours."

"Yeah, *Master*." Elliott's blue eyes were wide with mischief. "Besides, with the principal and the teachers at the party, Thorn and Bud won't dare make trouble. So there's nothing to worry about, *Master*."

The guys began laughing again.

"Okay, okay!" Finch agreed grudgingly. "We'll include them. But quit calling me Master." He tugged on the cape. "Except you."

They set up an assembly line. Elliott folded the paper. In black marker, Kev drew the bugles and lettered the word *Shhh*. With gold markers, Raj and Finch colored in the bugles. Everyone helped write out the insides:

Come to: A SURPRISE Birthday Party
For: Mr. Burns
Date: Friday, September 30
Time: 3:30 sharp!
Place: The Cafeteria
Please Bring a Birthday Card and a Snack to Share

"My hand hurts," Elliott complained when they were done.

"Mine, too." Raj waggled his fingers.

"How are we going to give them out without getting caught?" Kev asked.

Finch straightened the stack of cards. "I already

thought of that. Back to School Night is the perfect time. Mr. Kutler told me everyone's going to meet in the gym first. So while all the classrooms are empty, you guys can put an invitation on each teacher's desk. I'll take care of the invitations for our classmates."

"I love surprise parties," Elliott exclaimed. "I can't wait to see Mr. Burns's face when we all jump out."

I used to love parties, too. My master the merchant always held them on his birthdays. Everyone would dress in his or her finest clothes. The maid always washed and brushed me for the occasion. Do you think I need a washing, Master Finch?

"Wait a minute. I'm not wearing you to Mr. Burns's party," Fin said. "If I did, everyone at school would laugh at me."

But, Master, you might need me there.

"At a party? What for? This isn't the olden days. Ordinary guys don't wear capes. Besides, something could happen to you."

"Yeah, someone might spill a drink on you," Kev said.

"Or worse." With a flick of his wrist, Elliott flung something rubbery and yellow toward Finch. *Splat!* It hit him in the chest. The Thinking Cape let out a yelp.

Aiyyya!

Fin grabbed the rubbery mess. "Yeah, you could get hit by flying puke." He sent the fake vomit sailing back to Elliott.

The Thinking Cape was silent.

"What's the matter? Didn't they have fake vomit in old Persia?" El teased.

The guys hooted at the thought. But the Thinking Cape still didn't make a peep. And for once, it didn't talk to Finch all the way home.

NIGHT CLIMBERS

In the middle of the night, Finch awoke with a start. A chilly breeze blew over his blanket and made him shiver. "Cape?" He felt around his mattress. Had he kicked it onto the floor in his sleep? He'd stayed up late watching an old *Superman* movie he'd hoped would cheer up the Thinking Cape. But the cape hadn't seemed to enjoy the movie. It had hung limply over his shoulders. It didn't laugh at any of the funny parts.

Finch sat up and switched on his lamp. The Thinking Cape was draped over the sill, hanging half-way out.

"Cape, what are you doing up there?" he whispered as he snatched it back inside.

A swift breeze blew me up here, Master. I have been enjoying the fresh air.

"Did you stir up the wind again?" Suddenly Finch had a worrisome thought. "You weren't trying to get out, were you?"

Nay, Master. I was only thinking about the moving picture we watched. I have always wondered what it would be like to sail in the sky like that.

Finch felt his throat tighten. The cape sounded depressed. Maybe he wasn't doing such a good job of taking care of it.

"I could show you how it feels to be closer to the sky," he offered.

Really, Master?

"Yep, let's go." Finch stuffed his feet into his sneakers and tied the cape on over his pajamas. He grabbed his pillow, a flashlight, and his book and climbed out the window.

He was afraid someone might see the flashlight beam, so he trotted across the yard in the dark. He was used to running with his eyes shut anyway. When he got to the tree, he felt around the trunk for the wooden slats his dad had nailed up as toeholds. The breeze nipped at Fin's ears and the tip of his nose as he began climbing. But across his back, the cape felt as warm as a steam pipe.

"How do you like it?" Fin asked when they'd reached the wide, sturdy platform. He hadn't come up here since school had started. The crescent moon was like a big yellow smile in the sky. The treetops waved their leaves at him.

Now I know how a flying carpet feels, Master. It is wonderful!

Finch tied the cape to the railing so it could flap without sailing away. Then he lay on his back with his pillow under his head. "Would you like to hear a story from this book?"

Indeed, Master! Would you mind reading the one about the fisherman and the bottle again?

"Okay." It was one of Fin's favorites, too. The story was about a simple fisherman who found a copper bottle in his net as he dragged it from the sea one morning. Finch turned on the flashlight and began reading aloud.

"Although it won't fill our bellies, my wife might like this pretty vessel," the fisherman said. As he lifted it up, the bottle made a sound like the shifting of sand. The old man pulled out its stopper and turned it over. No sand poured out. Instead, a cloud of smoke rushed upward and a jinni appeared. It was so tall its head nearly reached the clouds, and so fierce its sword flashed brighter than lightning.

"Prepare to die, unlucky one," the jinni boomed.

At first, the fisherman just gaped at the jinni. Then he asked, "Where did you come from?"

"From the bottle, you stupid worm," the jinni replied.

The fisherman eyed the bottle. "I couldn't even get my big toe through that bottleneck. You could never fit in there."

"Are you saying I'm a liar?" the jinni raged. With his flashing sword he sliced at the sky.

The fisherman shrugged. "Only a fool would believe you could fit in that small container."

"You're the fool!" the jinni thundered. But though he stormed, and spat, and waved his sword, the stubborn fisherman still refused to believe him.

"I'll show you!" the jinni thundered. He turned into a cloud of blue smoke and wafted back into the bottle.

"Are you all the way in?" the fisherman asked.

"Yes, you numbskull," the jinni's voice echoed.

"Good, then I believe you," the fisherman said, and immediately pushed the stopper back into the bottle. With an arm that was strong from years of fishing, he threw it far into the sea. That was how a simple fisherman got rid of a boastful jinni forever.

"That's such a great story," Finch said as he closed the book.

But it is not true, Master.

"What do you mean?"

The fisherman was clever, but he did not dispose of the jinni forever. Sometime later, my master the merchant purchased the same copper bottle in a shop that sold antiquities.

"What are those?"

Ancient objects of interest, Master. The merchant wanted to add the old bottle to his personal collection. But as he was about to set it on a shelf that held three other bottles, he heard a sound like the shifting of sand. So he pulled out the stopper and turned it over.

Finch swallowed. "And the jinni appeared?"

Exactly so. Unfortunately, it was still horribly angry. It was ready to strike down my master with its terrible flashing sword.

"Quick, Master," I said. "Tell it there are also jinnis

in the other three bottles—one who claims it is the most powerful in the world, another who says it owns the largest diamond in the world, and the third who is the most beautiful female jinni in all the worlds of the universe."

In a shaking voice, my master did as I bade him.

"Is that so?" roared the jinni. "Well, any jinni who claims he is stronger than myself is a liar. And what do I care for diamonds, when I can take whatever I want from anyone, anywhere? But beauty is another story. I would like nothing better than a beautiful wife. Pull the stopper from her bottle and let me see her."

The merchant obeyed. Nothing appeared. The jinni raised his lightning bolt of a sword to slay him.

"Explain that the lady is shy because so many unworthy jinnis have tried to woo her, Master," I urged.

My master did so. His voice was so meek, the jinni had to stoop to hear it.

"Then I will enter the vessel to meet this lady—but only for a moment," the jinni grumbled with impatience. "When she sees how handsome I am, she will certainly come out with me. Wait here." And in an instant, he turned into a puff of red smoke and wafted into the bottle.

"Master, hurry! Put the stopper in," I instructed.

Quickly, my master closed up the bottle. Then he hired a boat and we set sail immediately. When we reached the center of the sea, my master tossed the copper bottle overboard. That is the true story of how the jinni was disposed of for good.

Finch thought for a moment. "If the jinni was so ferocious, why didn't he just kill the merchant before he went into the bottle to look for the female jinni?"

But that is the point, Master. With my help, the merchant outwitted him.

"Again? After being fooled by the fisherman? Huh! That jinni was a real dummy." Finch yawned. "I'm pooped. We'd better go back inside." He began gathering his stuff. He was about to start down the tree when he thought of something else. "Cape? In the book it said the jinni turned into blue smoke. But you said it turned into red smoke. Which was it?"

A jinni can turn into any color smoke it chooses. It is a small matter.

"Oh," Finch said. Maybe he was being picky, but there was something about the Thinking Cape's story that was bothering him.

BUSTED

"Do you really have to bring your backpack along?" Finch's mother asked as they left for Back to School Night. "What have you got in there, anyway?"

"Just some stuff I might need, like a pencil and pad to take notes," Finch answered.

"Fourth grade must agree with you. You're so diligent this year."

"What's that?"

"Hardworking. Careful."

"Oh—I've had a lot of help," Finch said.

His mother pulled him into a big hug. "I wish you'd give yourself some credit. But I'd also like an opportunity to thank your teacher—and whoever else has been helping you."

A crowd of parents and students were already walking down the hall as they entered the building. "We're supposed to go to the gym first," Fin said. "Mr. Kutler is going to welcome everyone." Out of the corner of his eye, he spotted his dad. He could hardly believe it! Even when his parents had still been married, his dad hadn't come to very many school events.

For the first time in years, he took his mother's hand. "This way, Mom," he said, towing her along.

"Fin, hold on!" his father called as he wove in and out of the crowd.

Finch pretended not to hear. He stuck out his chin and kept on going—or tried to.

"Finch, that's your dad. We have to wait." Mrs. Mundy began to slow down.

But Finch only tugged her harder. He hated having both parents together at the same time. He didn't know how to act. He was worried his mom might get upset. When his dad had moved out, she'd cried a lot. Why hadn't he stayed home with the blob?

"Finch, stop!" His mother planted her feet and refused to move.

"No rough play in the hallways!" a voice barked. A hand grabbed Finch's arm and yanked him around. Thorn flashed him the grin of a man-eating shark.

Finch stared at the name tag stuck to his chest. In red magic marker it said THORN—HOSPITALITY CAPTAIN.

"Is this a friend of yours?" Mrs. Mundy asked.

"Classmate" was all Finch could manage to say.

Thorn whipped a little notebook out of his back pocket and removed a pencil from behind his ear. "Sorry, but I've got to write your names down," he told Mrs. Mundy. "I'll have to report you."

"I'm a lawyer," Mrs. Mundy told Thorn. "If you do, I'll haul your butt into court."

Thorn's jaw dropped. "But you're supposed to obey the rules."

"I'm sure the rules say you're not allowed to touch anyone," Mrs. Mundy said. "Get going or I'll report you for Hospitality Abuse."

"I didn't hurt him," Thorn protested. But he began backing away.

"Mom, you're not a lawyer—you're an insurance agent," Fin said when Thorn was gone.

"And he's no hospitality captain," she answered. She giggled at her own joke.

Finch managed a weak smile. He knew she'd been trying to help, but his mother didn't understand. It was one more thing for the Thorpion to hold against him.

"Hello, Elaine." Suddenly Finch's dad was beside them. On the shoulder of his sport coat Finch noticed a crusty stain. It looked like baby food or spit-up. Probably his dad thought it was cute.

"Hello, Pete," Mrs. Mundy said, switching to the voice she used for business.

"How are you, buddy?" Mr. Mundy gave Finch a playful punch in the shoulder.

"Dad, what are you doing here?" Fin said accusingly.

His father opened his mouth but no words came out.

"Finnnnn." There was a warning in his mother's tone.

"I thought I'd find out what you'll be doing in school this year—and meet your new teacher," his father said.

Fin stared down the corridor. "Don't you have to be home with Jake?"

"Lisa is taking care of him."

"But you don't like coming to this kind of stuff," Fin said.

The tips of Mr. Mundy's ears were red. So were Fin's. "I want to be here, Fin. Is that okay?"

Finch shrugged. "It's a free country."

His mom put a hand on his shoulder. "Please, Fin. This isn't the time to—"

"It's all right," Mr. Mundy said quietly. "I'll just head over to the gym. I'll see you in your classroom after the principal's talk."

"I'm sorry, Pete. I guess Fin can't handle being with both of us together," Finch's mother said.

"Yes, I can!" Finch snapped.

Master Finch, you should give your father a chance to show you—

Finch elbowed his backpack. "Quit butting in," he ordered silently. "You're not my conscience."

But, Master. It is not too late to say you are—

"That's it," Finch murmured under his breath. "Pell-mell, a speechless spell!"

Suddenly he felt a tap on his shoulder. "Come on,

we'd better go, too," his mother said. The tightness in her voice made Finch wish he'd never heard of Back to School Night.

At the entrance to the gym, they stopped. The big square room was set up with rows of folding chairs. Already, most of them were full. Mr. Kutler was up front, adjusting a microphone.

Elliott and his mom arrived. "Hello, Elaine. Hello, Finch," Elliott's mother said.

"Hi, Ms. Levenson. Hi, El." Finch felt relieved that his mother would have someone to sit with. Ms. Levenson wasn't married either. She and Elliott, and their big dog, Peewee, lived in an apartment near the campus where she worked.

"I think there are some empty chairs all the way on the right," Ms. Levenson said. "We'd better take them before someone else gets there."

Finch squirmed uncomfortably. "I've got to go to the bathroom."

"Maybe I'd better go, too," Elliott said.

Mrs. Mundy frowned. "Mr. Kutler looks almost ready to start."

"That's okay, Mom. You and Ms. Levenson go

in. We'll see you later." Without waiting for her reply, Finch turned and ran. Elliott was right behind him. Finch was worried they'd run into Thorn or Bud, or one of the other hospitality captains. But they managed to get to the boys' room without being seen.

Kev and Raj were already there. "What took you guys so long?" Kev grumbled. He took the stack of invitations out of his backpack.

"Don't worry," Finch said, although his stomach was doing gymnastics. "We've got plenty of time. Mr. Kutler really likes to talk. While you're delivering the invitations around school to the teachers, I'll do the ones for the kids in our class. Meet me at our room when you're done."

He opened the bathroom door and peeked out. No one was in the corridor. "Okay, let's go!"

All the lights in the empty classroom were on when Finch arrived. As fast as he could, he stuffed an invitation into each of his classmates' desks. Then he went to his teacher's computer and tried the mouse. Good—Mr. Burns hadn't shut down yet. He clicked on the e-mail program. There was one more person he wanted to invite. It was a long shot, Finch knew, but if that person came, it would make the surprise party even more surprising.

To: Anthony Burns ABurns@mailme.com
Subject: Surprise Party

Dear Mr. Anthony Burns,
I'm a student at Middleburgh Elementary School. Your brother Mr. Slope Burns is my teacher. To help him feel at home, we are having a surprise party for his birthday. But I think the best surprise would be if you were here, too.

I am writing to you from your brother's e-mail account, but please answer me at Madbird@mailme.com so you don't spoil the surprise.

The party is here at school on Friday, September 30, at 3:30, seven days from now. I really hope you can come!

Sincerely,
Finch Mundy

Finch was clicking "Send" when he heard a voice outside the room. Quickly, he turned off the computer and hid in the kneehole space under the desk.

"Da da DAAA, da da DAAAH," the voice sang. It was the theme from *Rocky*. Finch's stomach dropped like a stone down a well. He knew whose voice it was.

THE INSURANCE POLICY

"Heh-heh! This is going to be great," someone else said.

Ugg. Finch knew who that was, too—the world's only talking dung beetle. He held his breath and listened as feet shuffled across the floor. They seemed to be heading toward the window.

"Hey, you crummy crabs, look at this nice shell. You both want it, don't you?"

"Heh-heh—guess you guys have got to fight for it."

Still on his hands and knees, Finch peeked around

the side of Mr. Burns's desk. Thorn was removing the screen from the top of the crabs' tank. Beside him, Bud was holding a big orange shell.

"Okay, put it in," Thorn directed.

Bud looked into the tank. "Do they bite?"

"Aww, is Buddy-Wuddy scared of the cwabby-wabbies?"

"No."

"Then do it!"

Clank! The shell clattered down between Phillip and Anthony. "Attack!" Bud ordered.

Instead of crawling toward the shell, both crabs backed away.

Thorn tapped the glass. "Come on—you're supposed to be crabs, not chickens. Fight for it!" He smirked at Bud. "I think we need to give them a little encouragement. Get some paintbrushes."

Bud ran to the Art table and grabbed two paintbrushes. "Here." He handed one to Thorn. "Now what? We paint 'em?"

Thorn rolled his eyes. "Do I have to tell you everything? Watch." With the back end of the brush, he pushed Anthony toward the new shell.

Anthony's antennae began going crazy.

Bud stuck his paintbrush into the tank, too. "Move it, Philly!" He used the brush like a drumstick to bop Phillip.

Little electric shocks were running down Fin's arms and legs. He had to stop Thorn and Bud before they really injured the crabs. But the Thinking Cape's warning was stuck in his brain: *A melon seed in the ground may one day reappear a thousand times bigger and fatter and pop you in the nose.* He imagined getting hit in the face by a big, round honeydew.

He didn't want to get hurt, but even more he didn't want to get into trouble. What if someone came in while he was fighting? Last time he'd gotten blamed. It could happen again. He'd already upset his mom enough tonight.

But Thorn had Anthony in his hand now. He was shaking him. "Come on out here, you spineless seafood, or I'll have to crack your shell open," he threatened.

Quietly, Finch crawled out of the kneehole. He held his breath until he was right behind the two hospitality captains. "Put him back!" he ordered.

Thorn jerked his head around. For a moment, he looked startled. Then he chomped his teeth together.

"Who's going to make me, Towelman? Your lawyer mommy?"

"No, I am."

"I thought you didn't believe in using your gift," Bud piped up.

"S-sometimes it's necessary." Finch thought about running out of the room to get help, but he didn't want to leave the crabs alone with Thorn and Bud for even a moment. He sent a frantic thought message toward the wall where his backpack was hanging. "Cape, I need help!"

The cape didn't reply.

Finch tried again. "Look, I'm sorry I told you to shut up before. I shouldn't have said it."

The stillness in Finch's head continued. Suddenly he remembered—the cape was under the speechless spell. "Quell, quell the—"

"What'd you say?" Bud asked before Finch was finished.

Fin bit his lip. "Er, I said 'ssspell.' I'm not sure how to spell, uh, *insurance*,'" Finch stammered.

Thorn squinted at Finch. *"Insurance?"*

"Yeah, *insurance*," Finch said as an idea formed in his head. "I'm trying to remember how to spell *insur-*

ance so I can write it down." He ran over to Mr. Burns's desk and grabbed a sheet of paper and a pencil.

"What are you doing?" Thorn snarled. He drew his arm back as if he were going to hurl Anthony like a baseball.

"Put him back!" Finch begged. "I'm going to fight you. I just have to write my insurance policy first."

"You're nuts, Towelman," Thorn said, but he put the crab into the tank.

Finch scribbled as fast as he could. When he was done, he shoved the paper across the desk. "Here, sign this and I'll fight."

Thorn held the paper up to read.

Insurance Policy

I certify that Finch Mundy is not responsible for my injuries because I made him fight me.

Signed ____________________

"Hurry up—sign," Finch urged.

"Why should I sign this?" Thorn dropped the sheet onto the desk.

"Insurance is a kind of protection in case something bad happens," Finch explained. He wasn't the son of the town's best insurance agent for nothing. "I need to protect myself in case I hurt you. I don't want to get expelled from school. My mom would go through the roof." Finch raised an eyebrow. "You met her. She can be pretty tough."

"Ha! You're not going to get expelled," Thorn said. "You're just going to get injured."

"If I hurt you really bad, I might." Finch glanced at the clock. "Better hurry and sign your name."

Thorn jabbed Bud with his elbow. "Buddy can say who started it."

"Oh, no." Finch shook his head from side to side. "I'm not trusting him. Besides, what if I knock him out, too?"

"Me?" Bud took a step backward.

"This is dumb. You're faking. You couldn't even knock yourself out," Thorn said.

"Then sign it and let's fight."

"First I'm taking out insurance, too." Thorn helped himself to a sheet of paper.

"You can't—you're the one who's insisting on fighting. I'm just going to defend myself," Finch pointed out.

Thorn crossed his arms over his chest. "Then I'm not signing."

Finch shrugged. "Okay, don't. But I'm leaving this on Mr. Burns's desk anyway."

"Give me that!" Thorn grabbed the paper and began tearing it into bits.

"Shh! Someone's coming," Bud whispered.

All three boys looked toward the door as the thundering of feet sounded in the hallway. Raj, Kev, and Elliott ran into the room.

"What are you guys doing here?" Thorn demanded.

"What are *you* doing here, *Thorpion*?" Kev shot back.

Thorn's eyes flashed rays of death at him. "I'm a hospitality captain. I'm keeping the school safe. You're not supposed to be here now." He pulled his notepad from his back pocket. "Too bad I'm going to have to report you guys for skipping Mr. Kutler's talk in the auditorium." He removed the pencil from behind his ear and began writing down their names.

"If you do, I'll tell Mr. Burns what you and Bud were doing," Finch threatened.

Thorn hesitated. "Guess we should call a truce, then." He held out his hand to shake. Suddenly a disgusted look came over his face. He brought his palm to his nose and sniffed. "Ew, it smells like crab poo—I'd better wipe my hand first." He leered at Finch. "Got a towel?"

"No!"

Bud began cackling. But Thorn was suddenly businesslike. "C'mon, Buddy, we'd better go to the boys' room and wash off the stink."

VANISHED!

"Oh, man! Why did Thorn ask for a towel? You think he knows something about the Thinking Cape?" Raj whispered as parents and kids began straggling into the room.

"Why would he? No one said anything, right?" Slowly, Finch peered into each guy's face.

"Don't look at me," El protested.

Fin glanced toward the side of the room. He could still see his jacket on the hook where he'd left it, and underneath, the bulge of his backpack. He wished he'd left the Thinking Cape at home—it was in a meddlesome mood. To be safe, he decided to keep the speechless spell in force.

Someone put a hand on his shoulder and squeezed. "Fin, where have you been?" his mother said. "You missed the principal's talk."

"Sorry."

"You were inexcusably rude to your dad. I don't know what's gotten into you tonight."

Finch studied the floor. He couldn't see why his mother was worrying about her ex-husband. He'd gotten himself a replacement wife and a replacement son. He didn't need them anymore.

His mother sighed. "Okay, we'll talk about it later. Why don't you show me around until your teacher gets here?" She pointed to the side of the room where Mr. Burns had filled a bulletin board with the compositions the students had written on their first day of school. "What are those?"

"Just some stuff we wrote. You don't have to read mine—it's not so good," Finch said quickly.

But Mrs. Mundy went over to look anyway. Finch trudged after her. "Where's yours?" she asked as she scanned the bulletin board.

Finch wished he'd chosen to write about the *Spider-Man* movie, which she'd taken him to, instead of the lookout platform he'd built with his dad. He glanced around. At least his father hadn't come to the classroom. Maybe he'd decided to go home.

But a moment later, Mr. Mundy came walking in with Mr. Burns. They looked as if they were having a serious discussion. Maybe his teacher was telling how Finch had disrupted the class with his "scorpion" outburst. Or maybe his dad was telling Mr. Burns about how he'd acted tonight in the hall. Either way, Fin felt like a bug under a microscope—a flea, or a tick, or a dung beetle.

"Good evening," Mr. Burns said in a formal voice that made some kids giggle. He was actually wearing a jacket and a tie. His bunchy red hair was all gelled down. "Students, please take your regular seats. Parents, you can pull one of the extra chairs over to sit with your kids. You're also welcome to sit along the windowsills and any other spaces you find."

Fin's mother brought a chair up beside his. To his relief, his dad leaned against the back wall. Once Mr. Burns began explaining about the activities at the learning centers, he sounded more like himself. Finch tried to listen, but his mind kept wandering. He'd have to remember to remove the shell Thorn had dropped into the crab tank without attracting attention to himself. He wondered if there was a way to attach an alarm to the tank in case the scorpion or the dung beetle stuck their hands in again.

Then there was the problem of the Thinking Cape. It was getting harder to keep it from being discovered. He knew some of it was his fault—he kept forgetting to speak to it inside his head. But the cape could be pretty annoying. It wanted to tell him what to do. It was oversensitive. It kept asking for things that were impossible, like being worn in public.

"Are there any questions?" Finch heard Mr. Burns ask. His presentation seemed to be over.

Mrs. Mundy raised a hand. "Are the students going to do a research project this year?"

"As a matter of fact, they're going to do one on extinct animals next month," Mr. Burns answered.

The idea of extinct animals always made Finch a little sad. He hated the notion that there had once been creatures he would never get to see except in a book or a museum. And he couldn't help imagining how lonely life must have been for the very last dinosaur, or dodo bird.

Probably, that was how the Thinking Cape felt. It wasn't an animal, but it was almost extinct, too. It could even have been the only one left on the planet. Suddenly Fin felt guilty. He promised himself he'd wear the cape around the house this weekend, even if Mimi made fun of him. He'd do other fun things for it too, like rent a new superhero DVD. And he'd take it up to the lookout platform to read more of *Tales from the Arabian Nights*. This time he wouldn't ask a single question if the Thinking Cape told a different version of the tale.

"Fin, time to go," his mother said, waking him from his thoughts.

He looked around. Everyone was leaving. Raj and Kev waved as they walked out with their parents. Elliott and his mom were already gone. "I'll get my things," he said, heading for the side of the room.

Chloe's stuff was hanging next to Fin's. "This was such a great idea to have kids come with their parents to Back to School Night," she said as she lifted her sweater off the hook. She was still wearing her hospitality captain badge. "I hope we do it again next year."

"Yeah, great," Finch grunted. He grabbed his sweatshirt and put it on. Then he lifted his backpack. He was slipping one of the straps over his shoulder when he realized something. It seemed too light.

"Hey, Cape, is everything okay?" he asked silently. He waited and listened in his head. The Thinking Cape didn't reply. He unzipped his pack just enough to slip a hand inside.

"Ahh!" Finch gasped, very much out loud.

Chloe giggled as if he were joking. "Did your backpack bite you?"

"No! I lost my . . . something." Finch could feel his ears flashing red.

"What?"

"My, er, homework notepad."

"Well, if you need the assignment, you can call me tomorrow. My mom calls me

Miss Organized." Chloe flashed Finch a big, bright smile. "Do you want my telephone number?"

"I'll look it up," he said stiffly.

"Okay. I've got to go now—my mom's waiting. Bye, Finny!"

Finch tried to smile, but he could only grit his teeth. He turned his back and peered into his pack.

"Fin, is everything okay?" his mother asked from behind him.

"No—my homework pad is missing."

Mrs. Mundy sighed. "Look around the floor. You probably dropped it somewhere."

Finch checked in the kneehole of his teacher's desk and under the table that held the crab tank. He looked on the bookshelves, in the Banking Center, and beneath the Art table. He even poked in the garbage can. "Quell, quell the speechless spell!" he chanted. "Cape, where are you?"

The only thing he heard was his own fast breathing.

His mother had her car keys out as she approached him. "Maybe someone picked it up by mistake. I'm sure whoever has it will return it Monday."

"No! I mean I need it to do my homework."

"It's Friday night. Tomorrow you can call one of

the guys for the assignment. Now let's go. It's getting late."

"I can't leave!' Finch yelled. "I've got to find it."

His father joined them. "Is something wrong, Fin?"

"My notepad is gone."

"I'm sure it will turn up," Mrs. Mundy said. "Don't be unreasonable."

Finch clenched his jaw and shook his head. "I need to keep looking."

"Elaine, if you want to go home, I'll search with him a little while longer," Mr. Mundy offered.

"Would you? Thanks. I'm bushed." Mrs. Mundy pecked the top of Fin's head. "See you later."

Fin and his dad traced the route along the corridor from the classroom to the gym. The custodian, Mr. Paul, let them into the front office to search the Lost and Found box. In the boys' room they checked the stalls. Fin didn't find the cape.

"I think we've looked everywhere. Let's go home, buddy," Mr. Mundy finally said.

Finch hung his head. He felt as if he were going to cry. As they walked out of the building, his father put an arm around him. "What was in your notepad, anyway? It wasn't just homework, was it?"

Something in his father's voice made Fin feel as though he could tell the truth. "I didn't really lose my notepad. I lost my cape."

"The old one with the lightning bolts?" His father looked surprised, but not like he thought it was funny.

"Yeah," Finch said. He didn't try to explain. To his relief, his dad didn't ask him to. They got into Mr. Mundy's station wagon and drove in silence for a while.

"Your teacher told me you're the first friend he's made here," Mr. Mundy said finally. "He thinks you have an unusual ability to empathize with people and hermit crabs."

"What does *empathize* mean?"

"It means you're a caring, understanding kid." Pete Mundy reached across and ran a hand over Fin's hair.

Fin felt like a giant rat. He couldn't believe his dad was saying nice things after the way he'd behaved tonight.

"I've got an idea. How about sleeping over at the apartment? Lisa makes great pancakes, and after breakfast, you and I could take Jake to the park. I could call your mom right now."

"I don't really feel like it tonight."

"Listen. I'm sorry I haven't shown it lately, but I think you're a really special kid. I know I've been wrapped up in Jake. I just wanted to give him a good start, so he grows up to be a superhero like you."

Fin closed his eyes. His dad had it wrong—he wasn't special. And without the Thinking Cape he definitely wasn't a superhero.

AN URGENT MISSION

At seven o'clock in the morning, Fin knocked lightly on Elliott's front door. "Hi, take off your shoes," Elliott whispered as he opened the door to his apartment. "My mom likes to sleep late on Saturday."

With one hand, Fin patted El's big golden retriever, Peewee. With the other he yanked off his sneakers. Then the boys slid down the narrow hall in their sweat socks. The dog trotted after them.

Raj and Kev were already in Elliott's room. The guys all knew about the missing cape. Finch had called them after his dad dropped him off, even though it was late.

"It's going to be okay," Raj said as Finch settled down by the door. "The cape survived for a thousand years. It can take care of itself till we get it back."

"I bet Thorn has it," Kev announced. "He was smirking when he asked if you had a towel, remember?"

Finch shrugged deeply. "But my backpack was in the classroom with us all the time. I don't see how Thorn could have taken the cape out without someone seeing him."

Raj extracted a deck of mini–playing cards from his pocket and displayed the jack of spades. "My magician's book says anything is possible through the art of distraction." He tossed the card up in the air and caught it. But when he opened his fist, the card had turned into the king of diamonds.

"Are you sure you brought the cape to Back to School Night?" Kev asked. "Maybe you forgot to pack it."

Finch nodded. "I'm sure. It was being kind of a pain."

"There's something I don't get," Raj said as he toyed

with a mini-card in his hand. "If the cape was being stolen, why wouldn't it have called you for help?"

Finch hung his head. "It couldn't. I got mad because it kept trying to make me apologize to my dad for something I'd said. So I put the speechless spell on it."

"But I still don't see why those guys would even look in your backpack," Elliott said as he rubbed Peewee's soft muzzle. "No one but us knew you kept the cape in it, right?"

Ugg! Finch squeezed his eyes shut as a memory flashed before him. "Bud came to Mimi's yard sale with his older brother, Ollie. He saw me put the cape in my backpack after it accidentally almost got sold. He might have heard me talking to it."

Kev leaped up. "Let's go over to Bud's right now. We'll make him give it back! If he doesn't have it, we'll go to Thorn's."

Raj adjusted his glasses on his nose. "We can't just knock on their doors and demand it without proof that one of them took it. Besides, we might only make things worse. They could decide to throw it away somewhere we'll never find it."

Finch had a vision of Thorn and Bud on a boat in the middle of the ocean. They were about to drop the cape into the water when a copper bottle floated up to the surface.

"I bet there's a jinni in there!" Thorn exclaimed. "If we catch it, we can make it give us three wishes."

The scorpion and the dung beetle flung the cape overboard so they could reach for the bobbing bottle. But before it hit the water, a gust of wind whipped up. Like a strange green bird, the cape was sent flying toward land.

"Yes!" Fin murmured.

Raj shook his shoulder. "Yes, what? Are you okay?"

Fin blinked. "Yeah. I was just thinking. You were right about the cape being able to take care of itself. But we're still going to get it back."

"How?" Elliott whispered.

"By doing what the cape would want us to do," Fin said. He'd never felt more certain or more determined in his life. "We're going to outsmart Thorn and Bud. We've got to."

"You got an e-mail," Mimi said when Fin got home. "Who is Anthony Burns? And what did he mean about a party?"

“You read my e-mail?” Finch pushed past her and ran to the computer room. His sister followed right behind him.

“So? What kind of secrets could you have?”

“None of your business!” Finch snapped. As soon as he’d said it, he knew he’d made a mistake.

Mimi’s eyes gleamed. “Oh yeah?”

Finch ignored her as he clicked on Anthony Burns’s message.

From: Anthony Burns ABurns@mailme.com

To: Finch Mundy Madbird@mailme.com

Date: Sat. 9/24

Subject: Surprise Party

Dear Finch:

Thanks for inviting me to the surprise party for Slope. Unfortunately, I’m planning to go camping then. It sounds like he’s going to have an awesome time without me, anyway. Ever since he was a kid, it’s taken him a while to get used to new situations. But if the other kids in class are as cool as you, I know my little bro' will have a great year.

Your friend in California,
Anthony Burns
P.S. Don't worry—I can keep a secret.

Finch closed the e-mail. Since the Thinking Cape had disappeared, he hadn't thought about the party at all. Suddenly he felt panicky. They hadn't just invited his class. They'd invited adults—every single one who worked at school. How could he have thought they could give a party for all those grown-ups?

"What's wrong?" Mimi asked.

Finch didn't answer. He knew what the Cape would say about trusting the "sour she-fruit." And then there was the Oath. The mission was supposed to be a secret. But he didn't have the Thinking Cape to help him now. He needed to talk to someone, even if it was his sister.

"Our teacher, Mr. Burns, is new here and he seemed kind of lonely. So the guys and I invited the kids in our class and all the adults in school to a surprise party for his birthday. I asked his favorite brother, Anthony Burns, to come, too."

Mimi rolled out her lip and stared at Finch. It made her look just like their mom. "You did?"

"Okay, it was a dumb idea."

"No, it wasn't—I think it was really nice," Mimi said. "I can't believe you thought of it."

"Gee, thanks. Anyway, his brother isn't coming. But what if everyone else does? I don't even know how to give a party."

"Of course you do. You've had one every year of your life. All you really need is cake and something to drink. The guests will know what to do."

Finch slapped his forehead. "I forgot about cake."

"I'll make cupcakes for you. Kelly will help me." Mimi reached out and messed his hair. "We owe you."

Finch shook her off. "You're kidding, right?"

"Doh—no," Mimi said, sounding exactly like Finch. "Don't worry. I'm not going to make it easy for you. You're going to have to wash the pans and bowls, and clean the counters, and take out the garbage, and sweep the floor. When I bake, I always make a really big mess."

"Wow, thanks," Fin said. But in spite of the smile he showed his sister, he felt a flush of shame inside. When the Thinking Cape had asked to go to the party, he'd turned it down. Now he would give anything for it to be there.

DROWNED HOPES

"Ms. Mitchell—did anyone turn in a green thing to the Lost and Found this morning?" Finch called as he hung over the counter in the school office.

The secretary looked up from her paperwork. "What kind of thing?"

Finch inspected an old mosquito bite on his arm. "It's sort of a towel with strings."

"And yellow lightning bolts," Elliott added.

"Oh, you mean a cape."

All four members of the SSSh stared down at their sneakers.

"I made one of those for my son Michael when he was little. His was blue and red."

The word *little* made Finch squirm.

Raj wiped at a speck on his glasses. "This one isn't for playing. It's a magician's cape."

Ms. Mitchell eyed him over the top of her own glasses. "Well, no one's brought in anything this morning. But it's early yet. Check back later." She looked down at her papers again.

The guys were almost at the door when Kev tiptoed back and slipped an envelope onto the counter. Inside was an unsigned note that that said:

> Dear Ms. Mitchell,
> Don't forget about the surprise party on Friday. Please call Mr. Burns to the cafeteria at 3:30. Thank you!

Next, the SSSh raced down the hall to their classroom. Mr. Burns was standing on his right leg with the left one bent so his foot rested against the inside of his thigh. "Hey, dudes, this is the tree pose," he said as they tumbled in. "Want to join me? We could be a forest together." He gave them an oversize wink.

"We thought we'd clean up the classroom," Finch said.

Without putting his left leg down, Mr. Burns dipped forward from the waist. As he straightened up, he looked at the guys' blank faces. "That was a tree bough—get it?"

Elliott, Raj, and Kev smiled weakly. Fin could only manage a slight nod. He wasn't in the mood for jokes right now. "We'll just get started," he said as he headed for the class ragbag.

"Hold on." Mr. Burns stared down his longish nose at the guys. "Did you forget that we cleaned up on Friday for the parents?"

Raj glanced around. "But it looks messy again."

"Yeah—I see a gum wrapper under there." Kev pointed toward the radiator.

"What are you guys—neatness fanatics? Well, if you want to, go right ahead." Mr. Burns changed legs and did a left-sided tree.

Raj got the broom. Elliott found the dustpan. Kev grabbed the wastebasket. Fin pulled a dust cloth out of the ragbag.

"Hey! What's that?" Elliott whispered, pointing under a cabinet.

Fin's heart leaped at the sight of a tiny corner of something green. He held his breath as Raj stuck the broom under the cabinet and fished it out.

It was only a dusty sheet of green construction paper.

"There's something behind here," Kev hissed, peering into the crack between the bookcase and the wall. He squeezed an arm into the narrow space. As his fingers reached the thing, a disgusted look appeared on his face. He drew out a half-eaten sandwich that was so green and hairy it looked like a science experiment.

Systematically, the guys cleaned under each student's desk and dusted the top. They also peered inside each one—except for Raj, whose job was to block the teacher's view as he swept. Elliott and Kev snickered whenever they saw something interesting—a squashed chocolate cupcake, a fist-size wad of chewed-up gum, comic books, a water gun. But Fin only moved on to the next desk without comment. Just as they were searching the last one, their classmates began trickling in. By that time, none of the members of the SSSh were smiling anymore. They hadn't found any sign of the Thinking Cape.

"Let's wait outside the door for Thorn and Bud,"

Fin said, although he wasn't sure what he was going to say or do when they arrived. He wanted to pop Thorn in the nose—on purpose this time. But he didn't have any proof that Thorn had stolen the cape. It was just a feeling.

As the room filled up, Finch looked at the clock. Where were Bud and Thorn? If they'd discovered the Thinking Cape could talk, they'd never keep it a secret. Once the news got out, the cape would become so valuable it would have to be locked up. It would hate that!

"What's going on over there by the door, dudes?" Mr. Burns called as the late bell started ringing. "Please take your seats now."

"I guess they're not coming," Elliott said as he and his friends headed toward their desks.

But a moment later, the scorpion and the dung beetle came hurrying in. Thorn hung his grungy gray backpack on a hook. But Bud carried his beetle-black one to his desk. Before he sat down, he looped one of the straps over the back of his chair.

Finch and Raj locked eyes.

"Oh, man, did you see that?" Raj hissed.

"Yeah—it's got to be in there!" Finch replied. It took all his self-control to remain in his seat. "Quell, quell the speechless spell! Cape, where are you?" he called silently. He held his breath and waited. "It's not answering," he told the guys.

"Maybe it can't talk," Elliott said. "Maybe it's injured."

"We've got to get a look in Bud's backpack," Raj whispered. He looked around. "But first, we need a distraction."

"That's easy." Elliott jumped up. "Uh-oh! The water in the goldfish bowl looks awfully low," he announced loudly. He dashed to the Critter Corner and grabbed the yellow plastic pitcher from the tray of supplies. In a moment, he was on his way out the door. Fin, Raj, and Kev shot one another puzzled looks.

Ms. Mitchell's piercing voice suddenly blasted over the loudspeaker. "Good morning. Today is Monday, September 26. Here are the morning announcements.

"Item one: Back to School Night was a great success. Students, please thank your parents for coming.

"Item two: If anyone found a green cape with yellow lightning bolts on Friday night, please bring it to the Lost and Found."

The classroom began to fill with snorts and giggles. Finch tried to look normal, but he could feel his ears turning red.

"Item three: Nurse Goldstein asked me to remind all students that health forms are due on . . ."

The classroom door banged open. "F.E.T.—Fish Emergency Technician coming through," Elliott shouted. The yellow pitcher was dripping as he hurried across the room. Water sloshed onto the floor as he rushed toward the fishbowl.

"Oops!" Just as he was passing Thorn's and Bud's desks, Elliott began to slip. He jerked back and forth, trying to catch his balance. Water splashed over the top of the pitcher.

"Watch it—" Bud reached out to push him away. But that only made Elliott more unsteady.

"Whoa!" he yelped as his right foot slid on a wet spot. The plastic pitcher flew out of his hand. Water spilled everywhere—but most of it landed on the scorpion and the dung beetle.

"You did that on purpose," Bud shouted as he tried to wring out his shirt.

"No, I didn't. It was an accident." Elliott was sprawled on the floor. "Look—I'm drenched."

"My pants are wet!" Thorn yelled.

Chloe, Zoe, and Kayla giggled.

Thorn shot them the rays-of-death glance. "Shut up!"

Flaaah! Flaaah! Flaaah! Mr. Burns's lungs were in good shape this morning. "Everyone chill out! Thorn, Bud, and Elliott—go to the nurse's office. She keeps extra clothes around for accidents."

At the word *accidents* some of the girls began tittering again—until Mr. Burns lifted his bugle. "Will someone go and get the mop from Mr. Paul?" he asked.

Finch jumped up. "I will."

"I'll get the pail," Kev volunteered.

"We'll need some towels," Raj said.

"Thanks, dudes. What would I do without you?"

While Finch and Kev mopped up the floor, Raj dried the desks with the old gray towel he'd gotten from Mr. Paul. No one noticed as Raj the Remarkable slipped Bud's backpack off his chair and rolled it up in the towel. It was like after the ambulance leaves the scene of the accident. The interesting part was over.

Before they returned Mr. Paul's supplies, the guys stopped in the boys' room. Raj unwrapped Bud's backpack from the towel. "Here, Fin."

"You look. I can't."

Raj nodded solemnly. "Okay." His slender brown fingers undid the buckles and slipped inside. One by one he removed:

- a library book on sharks
- a juice box (grape)
- a half-eaten granola bar (peanut butter)
- a spelling test (marked with an F)
- a math test (marked with a D)
- a crumpled note

Elliott grabbed it and smoothed it out.

Buddy,
Dad wants us to rake the lawn and bag the leaves after school, but I'm too busy. YOU DO IT!

Ollie

P.S. If you tell Dad I didn't help, I'll kick your butt to the moon.

Elliott whistled. "No wonder Bud is so mean."

"Are you sure there's nothing else in there?" Finch took the backpack and lifted it up. He turned it over and gave it a few hard shakes. Only a paper clip and a pen fell out.

Thorn and Bud were in their seats when the guys got back to the classroom. Bud gripped the edge of his desk at the sight of Finch carrying his backpack.

"Here—I dried this off for you," Fin said as he handed it over.

"Gimme that!" Bud's arm shot out and grabbed the pack. The sleeves of his borrowed gray sweatshirt were too long.

Thorn got halfway out of his chair to lean across his desk. He was wearing wide brown pants like the ones the custodian wore. With his broad chest and spiked yellow hair, Thorn looked like a cross between SpongeBob and Dracula.

"You and your towelboys think you're smart, but guess what? Buddy and I've got a surprise for you."

"What is it?" Fin asked before he could stop himself.

Thorn's big, closed-mouth smile made Fin's heart shrink. "You'll find out. And I can't wait to see your ferret face when you do."

A SURPRISE FOR THE SURPRISERS

On Friday morning, Finch and Raj stood in the corridor collecting everyone's birthday cards. Kev and El took the snack contributions and brought them to the cafeteria. The lunch ladies, Ms. White and Ms. Baker, had agreed to keep all the food in the kitchen until it was time for the party.

"How come you're in charge?" Chloe asked as she handed Fin her card.

"Chloe, this is awesome!" he said as he peered at her creation. She'd drawn a classroom full of puppies smiling at a grown-up teacher dog. The teacher dog was holding a giant bone with a red bow tied around it. Beneath the picture it said, *Hope you have a gnaw-some birthday!*

Chloe beamed. "Thank you. I thought of it myself." She'd already forgotten about her question.

At lunch, the guys picked at their sandwiches until everyone went out for recess. Then they blew up two packs of balloons and taped them to the columns around the cafeteria. Along the wall opposite the windows they stretched a line of string and hung their classmates' cards from it with paper clips. One of the cards had a picture of a round-faced character with spiky yellow hair and pointy yellow teeth. Inside, it was signed, *From Guess Who?*

"Those decorations make me feel like partying," Ms. White called from the kitchen, where she and Ms. Baker were washing pans.

"I may have to start dancing," Ms. Baker agreed. "Look out, boys, or later I'm going to ask one of you to be my partner."

"It's a good thing we're not having music," Elliott said.

Since Monday, Fin had hardly thought of anything but the Thinking Cape. But now, in spite of his worries, he felt a little spark of excitement. He imagined Mr. Burns's amazement when he walked into the party at 3:30. Just like a DON'T WALK sign, his face would start flashing red. Then he'd get this big grin on his face and his head would bobble like a balloon. The thought made Finch smile for the first time in days.

Ten minutes before three o'clock dismissal, a whisper got passed around Mr. Burns's classroom. No one was sure who started it.

"When the bell rings, leave the building as if you're going home. Wait ten minutes. Then come back in through the side entrance and go to the cafeteria."

Bzzzzzzzzzzzzzzzzzzzzzzz!

In an orderly fashion, the students filed out of the room. No one pushed, shoved, shouted, or even talked. Mr. Burns didn't seem to notice his students' unusually quiet behavior.

The members of the SSSh raced straight to the cafeteria. Kev and Raj arranged the snacks on one of the long tables. Elliott brought out the containers of lemonade they'd stored in the school's giant refrigerator.

"Is one of you named Finch Mundy?"

Finch looked up from setting out paper cups and plates.

A tall guy in a jacket, baseball cap, and black high-tops was standing in the doorway. He was holding a tower of pizza boxes—ten or twelve of them. "Delivery for you," he said.

Finch blinked at the tall stack. He'd never seen so many pizzas before. "I didn't order those."

"No?"

The man put the boxes down on the closest table and pulled out a receipt. "It says here, 'One dozen pizzas for Finch Mundy.'"

What kind of trick was this? Finch wondered. Could it be the surprise Thorn had threatened him with?

"B-but I can't p-pay for them," he stammered.

The man grinned. "They're already paid for. See?" He held out the receipt as he approached. There was something familiar about his walk. Then he took off his baseball cap. Underneath was a head full of bright red hair.

Finch's heart began doing jumping jacks. Could it

be? "Anthony?" he croaked. "I mean, are you Mr. Anthony Burns—Slope Burns's brother?"

"You've got that right, dude. Are you the Madbird?"

Raj, Kev, and Elliott all stared, openmouthed.

"B-but I thought you weren't coming," Finch blurted out.

Anthony Burns ducked his head. "To tell the truth, I've kinda been missing my little bro'. And I couldn't stop thinking about how cool it was that you kids were making him a party. I couldn't stand to miss it. So I decided to surprise the surprisers. Is that okay?"

"Sure," Finch replied quickly. But underneath his happiness, he was having a worrisome thought. He'd lost the Thinking Cape and gained Mr. Burns's brother. What if it was some kind of magical trade?

MAKE A WISH

"Slope Burns, there's a teachers' meeting in the cafeteria. You're late!" the loudspeaker squawked as Ms. Mitchell made her announcement.

The crowd of teachers and kids in the cafeteria laughed. Then someone hissed, "Shhhh!" in a loud voice.

"Should we hide?" Principal Kutler asked.

"In the kitchen!" Ms. Baker suggested.

"Don't run," Nurse Goldstein admonished.

Everyone scurried to the back of the cafeteria and

slipped into the long, narrow kitchen. Ms. White stayed behind to shut out the lights. In another moment, they heard footsteps racing down the hall.

"I'm sorry, I must have missed the announcement. I didn't know about today's meeting. Hello? Isn't anyone here?"

"SURPRISE!!!!!!!!!"

Ms. White snapped the lights back on. Students, teachers, and other school staff members flooded into the cafeteria, shouting "Congratulations!" and "Happy birthday!"

Mr. Burns's face grew flushed, just as Finch had imagined. "This is awesome. Thank you!"

"There's one more surprise," Ms. Mitchell announced. Even without the loudspeaker her voice was piercing.

"Shhhh! Shhhh!" Everyone shushed one another again. All heads turned to the back of the cafeteria as Anthony Burns walked in.

"Happy birthday, little brother," he said.

"Anthony—you're here!" Mr. Burns's jaw dropped. His head bobbled. And his eyes were glistening. Finch hoped his teacher wasn't going to start crying. He felt sort of choked up himself.

The two brothers grabbed each other. Anthony actually lifted Slope off his feet. The party guests gathered around them, laughing and clapping.

The members of the SSSh headed for the snack table. Finch and Kev poured lemonade. Elliott and Raj began putting pizza on paper plates as a line of hungry partygoers formed in front of them.

Thorn cut to the front. "I don't want your grubby fingers on my pizza, towelboys," he said. He reached into the box with both hands and grabbed a slice in each fist.

"Hey!" Elliott protested.

Quickly, Thorn bit into both slices. "What? Want me to put one back?" Cheese was dripping from his vampire fangs.

Bud cut in right behind him and reached into the box. But before he could get the other hand in, Raj closed the cover. "One to a customer," he said.

"Yeah, move it, Budster," Chloe added. She was next in line.

After everyone had been served, Ms. White ambled over to the snack table. "You boys are doing such a good job, I just may retire," she joked. She leaned over and whispered, "Did one of you bring candles to put in your teacher's cupcake?"

"Oops—I left them in my desk. I'll go and get them."

Finch didn't think it was necessary to admit that his sister was the one who'd remembered candles.

"I'll come with you," Elliott volunteered.

They crept past Mr. Burns and exited the cafeteria. The moment they were out of sight, they raced to the classroom door—and stopped short. Someone was already in the room. *Someones.* Carefully, they peeked around the doorframe.

"How's it look, Buddy?"

"Awesome."

Thorn and Bud were at the Art table. Thorn was holding a brush dripping with red paint. Spread out in front of him was the Thinking Cape. Straight across its middle, Thorn had painted TOWELMAN in big, crooked letters.

Fin's breath caught in his throat. "Cape, can you hear me?" he asked silently.

Yes, Master Finch.

"Where have you been? I've called you a million times!"

I am sorry, Master, but the scorpion stole me from your backpack and took me to his house. There he kept me hidden in the bottom of his closet under a heap of dirty clothes. Now I smell worse than camel breath.

"Don't worry. We can wash you at home," Finch said.

Nay, Master. By then it will be too late. The dung beetle has a scissor. Soon I will only be fit for dust rags. Good-bye, Master Finch. You have been good to me. Good-bye, Elliott. I know now that when you played your false-vomit joke on me, you were treating me as a friend.

"Don't give up! Think of something, Cape!" Elliott urged.

"El, do you have the vomit with you?" Finch whispered.

"Sure—I always carry it in case of emergency. It's in a brown paper bag in my backpack."

"Okay, then cross your fingers and let's go," Finch said. He ran into the classroom.

"Do we have to?" Elliott asked. But he followed behind Fin anyway.

"Hey, guys!" Finch shouted. "We've been looking all over for you."

"Hold on!" Thorn waved his brush. "I'm not done yet, Towelman."

"Yeah. We still have more work to do." Bud snipped the air with the scissors.

Fin waved a hand. "There's no time! You've got to come back to the cafeteria. Everyone's waiting for you."

Thorn squinted at him. "Why?"

"The kids voted for you to do the presentation."

"Huh?"

"You're supposed to give the class gift to Mr. Burns."

"Class gift?"

"Yes—it's in Elliott's backpack." Fin looked over his shoulder. "Hurry up, El, go get it," he urged.

The look in Elliott's eyes said, "Are you crazy?" But he went over to the wall where his backpack was hanging and took out a crumpled brown bag. "Here you go," he said as he brought it to Thorn.

Carefully, Thorn took it from Elliott's fingers. "The class really picked me?" For a moment, he looked as stunned as if he'd just been given the Good Citizenship Prize during the school awards assembly.

"Yeah—everyone thinks you have a nice speaking voice," Elliott said without meeting his eyes.

"Right," Fin agreed. "You're supposed to make a little speech when you give the gift to Mr. Burns."

Thorn narrowed his pale eyes. "You didn't say I have to make a speech."

"Just a little one," El said quickly. "Just something about how we're all glad Mr. Burns is our teacher because he makes learning fun."

"That's kiss-up talk," Bud sneered. He brought the scissors toward his puckered lips as if he were going to kiss the blades.

"Wh-why don't you put those away," Fin stammered. "We're not fighting anymore. R-right, Thorn?"

Thorn ignored him. "What's in here?" he asked as he weighed the bag on his palm.

Finch and Elliott looked at each other.

"It's, er, science equipment." Finch patted his stomach. "A rubber replica of the digestive system."

Thorn shot him a sideways glance. "What kind of present is that?"

"Mr. Burns is a teacher. That's the kind of stuff they like to get," Elliott said as if it were obvious.

Bud stuck his tongue out. "Yuck. I'm never going to become a teacher."

"Shut up, Buddy." Thorn tucked in his shirt. "I never got elected for anything before. Everyone always picks guys like you." He pointed a finger at Finch.

"Well, congratulations." Fin felt a flicker of regret. He wished the class really had picked Thorn for something. He wondered if that was what his dad had meant by empathizing.

"Yeah, whoopee for you." The dung beetle was still holding the scissors. The crazy look in his eyes made Finch feel queasy.

"You got picked to do something, too, Bud," he said quickly. "You get to carry the cupcake with the candles in it." He ran over to his desk and took out the candles his sister had given him. "Here."

"Just a sec—I'm almost finished." Bud lifted up one of the cape's satin ties.

"Come on. Put the scissors down," Finch urged.

"I said in a sec." Bud slipped the tie between the blades of the scissors.

"Stop!" Finch yelled as Bud closed the blades.

"Why?" Bud asked as he snipped off the other tie. He looked up and grinned. "Okay, I'm done. Hand over the candles and let's go."

Finch felt as if the blades had snipped something inside him. The pain was so sharp, he could hardly breathe. "First give me that," he wheezed. "You've already ruined it anyway." Gently, he lifted up the Thinking Cape and picked up its severed strings. For once the scorpion and the dung beetle were silent as he tucked the cape into his backpack.

THE PRESENTATION

Ms. White snapped off the lights once more, and everyone began singing "Happy Birthday." Walking as solemnly as if he were in a wedding procession, Bud carried a chocolate cupcake with a flaming candle toward Mr. Burns. Thorn followed behind him, cupping the paper bag in his palms the way he might carry something delicate and precious.

"I can't believe you told the scorpion there was a present in that bag," Kev murmured while everyone was singing. "Wait till he finds out what's really in there."

Finch shrugged. He wasn't afraid. He felt numb.

"Make a wish, Slope," Ms. Mitchell squawked.

Mr. Burns closed his eyes. So did Finch. He made a wish even though the candles weren't his.

The group clapped and whistled. When they were finished, Thorn stepped forward. "Everyone thinks you're a really great teacher. You make learning fun—sort of . . ."

Some of the kids began to snicker—until the scorpion shot them a glance that melted the smiles off their faces.

". . . so I thought to show our appreciation, we should throw a surprise party for your birthday, and get you this gift." Thorn grinned at Mr. Burns. "It's educational."

The rest of the students gazed at one another. Then they began whispering.

"Shut—I mean, be quiet!" Thorn commanded. He didn't need a bugle. No one spoke another syllable. He held out the paper bag. "I hope you like it."

"Thank you, Thorn. Thank you, everyone." Mr. Burns unrolled the top of the bag and glanced inside. Then he looked up at the guests. Once more he peered into the bag. This time he brought it closer to his face.

"Uh-oh—I think I feel sick," he said as he swayed

on his feet. "Too much pizza." He grabbed his brother's shoulder to steady himself. Then he bent in half and began heaving into the bag.

Thorn's grin froze. He stood there stiffly as if he didn't know what to do.

Suddenly Mr. Burns straightened up. With a quick flick of his wrist, he turned the bag over and shook it. A big splat of yellow vomit fell onto one of Thorn's sneakers.

"Yeee-uck!" Thorn jumped in the air. The vomit flew off his shoe and bounced twice on the floor. For a moment, he stared at it. "Rubber vomit," he said slowly.

Mr. Burns and his brother began whooping with laughter. The crowd around them joined in.

"Anthony and I used to have one just like this," the teacher said when he could finally talk. He scooped the rubber vomit off the floor and waved it around. "Kids, this is the best present you could have given me. You guys are great." He reached over and clapped Thorn on the back.

"Glad you like it," Thorn said. The look on his face wobbled from smile to frown and back again.

"Oh, man! Did you see the scorpion jump?" Raj gave his own jump of joy.

Kev was still cackling. "Yeah, the only thing better would have been if Mr. Burns really did spew on his sneaker."

"Come on, let's go get cupcakes before they're all gone," Elliott said.

"Save one for me," Finch said. "I've got to go back to our room and check on the cape."

THE TRUTH ABOUT THE GIFT

At exactly 10:30 on Saturday morning, the doorbell rang. It was Finch's dad.

"I've got the goods," Pete Mundy said as he patted the pocket of his jacket. "Where's the victim?"

"In my room." Fin led the way. Rosie and Cubby scampered along with them. Whenever Mr. Mundy came over, they got really excited.

Even though his mother was out selling insurance and his sister was at her dance lesson, Finch closed the door to his room. If one of them came home early, he didn't want to have to explain. He hadn't mentioned the Thinking Cape's injuries to either of them.

The cape was spread out on Fin's bed with the green satin strings beside it. The red painted slur, TOWELMAN, was gone. Fin had gotten Mimi to show him how to use the washing machine by saying that the ferrets' favorite blanket needed freshening.

"Hello there," Pete Mundy said, gazing down at the cape. "Mind if I inspect your injury?" He lifted a corner of the cape and examined the place where a string had been attached.

Finch tugged at the neck of his T-shirt. He hadn't told his father that the cape had been able to talk before Bud cut off its ties. Was his dad teasing, or did he suspect something?

But a moment later, Pete Mundy turned to Finch and wiggled his ears. "He's kidding," Finch told himself. He felt both relieved and disappointed at the same time.

"Now just hold still and this won't hurt a bit." Mr. Mundy reached into his pocket and pulled out a spool of green thread and a needle. Then he sat down on the bed and pulled the cape onto his lap.

Finch hung over his father's shoulder and watched him reattach the ties with neat, tiny stitches.

"That should do it," Mr. Mundy said as he made a final knot. He bit the end of the thread off with his teeth. "Here, try it on."

Finch tied the strings carefully. Slowly, he looked up at his dad.

"It still looks terrific on you—better than ever."

Finch felt the muscles in his upper arms twitching. He hadn't hugged his father since Jake was born. It was almost as though he couldn't anymore. But now the entire upper half of his body—chest, shoulders, neck, chin—seemed to be lifting up. Next, his arms floated out. They wrapped themselves around his father's middle.

Instantly, his father's arms grabbed him, too. Finch laid his head against his dad's shirt. He felt like he was melting. "Thanks, Dad," he whispered.

"Anytime, Fin." His father continued to hold him tightly. "Would you like to come home with me? You could teach your little brother to belch or something."

Finch laughed. "I'd like to. But could it wait till next weekend? There's something I have to do today."

"You're really going to come next weekend?"

"Yep. Promise."

"Cape, how do you feel now?" Finch asked the moment his dad was gone. He held his breath and waited. But he already knew it wasn't going to answer. He could feel it inside—or, rather, he could feel its absence. It was as if his head were a room, and there was an empty place where the sofa used to be.

Finch stood in front of the mirror on his closet door and gazed at himself in the cape. He didn't get it. How could scissors have destroyed its power if only the ties had been cut? The same thing had happened a thousand years before at the merchant's. Yet its voice had returned when the mother who'd made it into a cape for her son had sewed on its ties. Why couldn't it speak now that his dad had stitched them back on? Something else had to be wrong.

An idea came to him. He left a note for his mom and Mimi in case one of them got home first. It said, *Gone Biking.* Then he tied the cape tightly around his neck and went out the door. "I think you're going to enjoy this. It will feel a little like flying," he said as he wheeled his bicycle out of the garage.

If his mother had been aware of what he was doing, Finch knew she would not have approved. A few times she'd allowed him to ride into town with the guys—but never alone.

"I'm not alone—the Thinking Cape is with me," Finch argued in his head as he strapped on his bike helmet. But he wasn't sure it was true anymore.

As he pedaled past Raj's house, he slowed down. Calm, thoughtful Raj could be counted on for moral support. It would be nice to have him riding alongside. But Finch kept on going. He needed to do this himself. Since school had begun he had depended on the Thinking Cape. Now it was depending on him.

The traffic was heavier in town, so he walked his bike on the sidewalk. People were looking at him—a big boy in a superhero cape. Underneath his bike helmet, he felt his ears getting hot. He knew when he took it off he was going to look as if he had a blinking light on either side of his head. But he was determined to go through with his plan, no matter how embarrassing things got. He looked straight ahead and kept on going until he reached the video store.

"Do you have any movies about Persia or Arabia?" he asked the teenager at the counter. "Something that has a desert and camels?"

The guy jerked a thumb. "Try *Aladdin*. The kiddie section is over there."

Finch clenched his jaw. "I want something for adults."

"*Lawrence of Arabia*. Classics. Aisle three."

"Okay," Finch muttered. He was glad to disappear down the long, empty aisle. He took his time looking at titles before he pulled *Lawrence* off the shelf. The case cover had a picture of a guy dressed in flowing white robes sitting on a camel. He read the synopsis on the back. The story had something to do with the Arabs fighting the Turks for freedom. It sounded complicated, but he didn't really care about the plot. If the Thinking Cape was suffering from extreme homesickness, seeing its old homeland might wake it up. At least it was worth a try.

"You're in for a great surprise," he murmured as he approached the counter again.

"What'd you say?" the teenager asked.

"Nothing."

The door to the shop opened. Chloe, Zoe, and Kayla walked in. They stared at Finch.

"You get that cape for Halloween?" Kayla asked finally.

Finch took a deep bow. "Secret Superhero Fin Mundy at your service," he said.

The girls giggled.

"No, really. Are you going to a costume party?" Zoe asked.

"This isn't a costume. I just like wearing it. A thousand years ago lots of important guys wore capes."

Kayla pursed her lips. "Oh yeah?"

"I think George Washington wore one when he crossed the Delaware River. I saw a painting of it in the museum," Chloe said. She smiled at Finch.

"That wasn't a superhero cape," Kayla said.

The guy behind the counter handed Finch his change and a plastic bag with the DVD.

"What did you rent?" Chloe asked.

Finch slipped *Lawrence of Arabia* out of the bag. "I'm watching it with a friend of mine who used to live in the desert."

"Who?"

"Er, he's called T.C. You don't know him." Finch began backing toward the door. "Well, see you in school on Monday." He gave a last quick bow. It seemed to be becoming a habit.

Outside, Finch hung the bag on a handlebar and put his helmet back on.

"Hey, look who's here, Buddy—Towelman. But what happened to the sign I painted on his cape? I bet his lawyer mommy washed it off."

"Yeah. She must have sewed the strings back on, too."

It was finally coming true, Finch thought. His worst nightmare. Yet he felt strangely calm. He would wear the Thinking Cape in front of a stadium full of bullies if that would bring it back to life.

"I bet you and your friends thought you were really funny, giving me that bag of rubber vomit," Thorn said. "Don't think because Mr. Burns actually liked the stuff, you're getting away with it."

Bud blew a big bubble with his gum and popped it. "Yeah, you're busted now, Towelman."

Finch kept quiet. He nudged up his kickstand and got on his bike. Just as he was about to push off, a hand grabbed the back of the Thinking Cape. "Hey! I'm talking to you."

"Let go," Finch said in a quiet voice.

"Make me." The hand yanked the cape harder. "It's time to put up or shut up. Let's see your gift."

Finch reset his kickstand and got off the bike. "No," he said.

Thorn cocked his head. "No? Then hand over the cape."

"No," Finch said again. He was supposed to solve problems by thinking, not fighting—except he didn't have any idea how. Still, he felt determined not to break the Oath. In a way, it was all that was left of the Thinking Cape.

The door to the video store opened. Chloe, Zoe, and Kayla appeared on the sidewalk.

"Look—I caught a superhero," Thorn told them. He gave the cape another hard yank.

Finch grabbed his neck as the ties cut into his throat.

"Stop that!" Chloe demanded.

"Who's going to make me? Not Finch. He's just a baby in a super-blankie." Suddenly Thorn grinned. He pulled Finch closer. "Say it! Say you're a baby in a super-blankie."

Finch looked at the girls. They were all staring at him with their big, soft eyes. He felt as if two hands were wringing out his gut. "I'm a baby in a super-blankie," he murmured.

"Louder!"

"I'M A BABY IN A SUPER-BLANKIE!" Finch shouted. He felt a tear drip down his face.

Thorn looked away. "Okay, you can go now," he muttered as he opened his fist.

Bud spit his gum into his palm. "Yeah, move it—and take this with you." He reached out to slap the sticky wad onto the cape.

"No!" With superhuman speed, Finch's arm shot out and shoved him away. Bud's eyes and mouth were wide with surprise as he was propelled backward. Thorn was so busy gaping he didn't get out of the way fast enough. *BAM!* Bud crashed into him. Together the dung beetle and the scorpion toppled onto the pavement.

As Finch rode off on his bike, he could hear the girls clapping.

ONE LAST TRY

Mimi was already home when Finch came in the door. "You wore that thing outside?" she squeaked.

Finch shrugged. "The yellow lightning bolts really stand out in traffic."

"In traffic? Where'd you go?"

Finch held up the plastic bag.

"The video store! Mom's going to be furious when she hears you rode your bike into town."

"Not if you don't tell her." Finch put his hands together. "Please."

"I'll think about it." Mimi snatched the note off the

table and crumpled it up. "All of your friends called you. And Elliott called twice. What's going on?"

"Nothing." Finch filled a glass with water and emptied it in three gulps. "Do you want to watch the movie with me?"

Mimi looked in the bag. "*Lawrence of Arabia*? No thanks. Anyway, Kelly is coming over. We've got a school project to do." She scooped up Rosie and headed toward her room.

It was just what Finch had been counting on. When he heard her door click shut, he put on the DVD and settled on the living-room floor. Cubby climbed up on his shoulder and nuzzled his ear.

Lawrence of Arabia was a sad movie. Tons of soldiers died. So did tons of camels.

"Do you recognize any of these places?" Finch asked the cape after Lawrence had crossed miles of desert. "Does the sand really look that wavy? Did you ever see one of those scorpions?"

But the Thinking Cape was as silent as the drapes on the window.

"I don't think you're enjoying this. I'm not either. Personally, I'm sick of fighting," Fin said. As if he agreed, Cubby climbed down from his shoulder and skittered away. Finch shut off the DVD player and trudged to his room. Nothing was working. He didn't know what else to do.

He sank down on his bed—and sat on a book. From under the blanket he pulled out *Tales from the Arabian Nights*. He'd forgotten to return it to the library. He was still the same old Fin.

"You want to hear a story?" he asked the cape. He didn't wait for it to answer. "Mimi, I'll be out in the yard," he yelled.

From up on the lookout platform, Fin gazed at the sky. Thick gray clouds were rolling in fast. A cold breeze blew through the treetops. He pulled the cape tighter around him and opened the book. "The Second Voyage of Sinbad the Sailor," he began.

This time, ferocious, monkeylike pirates attacked Sinbad's ship. They left him and his crew on a strange island. "At least they didn't kill us," Sinbad said as the monkey-pirates sailed away.

Finch groaned. He knew more trouble was coming.

Sinbad led the crew on an exploration of the island. They didn't meet any people. But they did find the tallest gates they'd ever seen. Through the gates stood a vast white palace. "Let us go in and see what kind of people live there," Sinbad suggested.

Finch groaned again. He could already guess what kind of people lived there. Bad ones.

As soon as Sinbad and his men entered the courtyard, the gates locked behind them. They went up to the palace door and knocked until their knuckles were bruised. No one answered. The hungry, exhausted sailors picked coconuts for dinner and fell asleep on the open ground.

In the middle of the night, the palace doors creaked open. Out stomped a giant—a cannibal giant. He was hungry, too—but not for coconuts. He began munching down sailors as fast as if they were French fries.

Fin stopped reading. "I bet you and your old master visited this island, Cape. And I bet you weren't dumb enough to sleep out in the open, either. You probably hid until you saw who lived in the palace. Then you figured out how to steal the giant's treasure and escape with it. Right, Cape?"

The leaves whispered. The tree branches creaked. The Thinking Cape was silent.

Fin closed the book. It was time to face it—all he had around his shoulders now was some old green cloth. The Thinking Cape was gone for good. He pulled his knees to his chest and leaned his forehead against them.

"I'm sorry I didn't do a better job taking care of you," he murmured. "I warned you, didn't I? I told you I'd let you down. You should have let me give you away to someone more responsible. You shouldn't have trusted me."

Nay. It is you who should not have trusted me.

Underneath the cape, Fin's shoulders trembled. "Cape?"

I am here. But I am not worthy enough to call you Master.

"Why? What do you mean?"

I never visited the Valley of Diamonds. I never out-witted the jinni of the copper bottle.

"So you exaggerated. That's okay. I do it too sometimes."

I wish that were all, but there is more.

"You can tell me," Finch whispered. "I'll understand."

You may find the truth unforgivable.

"I've got to know, anyway."

Finch felt a flutter across his back as if the cape were sighing. For a moment, it was silent again. Then it began its final story.

THE CAPE'S SECRET

From the day you first called me the Thinking Cape, almost everything I have spoken is a lie. I am not a cape at all. Though my cotton was grown in the cape makers' secret field, I was made into a towel for the weavers to dry their hands on when they washed before the midday meal.

"What? You're only a towel!" Finch was stunned—and disappointed. But most of all he felt angry. The cape, or towel, or whatever it was, had fooled him. It had lied.

I am sorry, but it is true. Day after day, I hung beside the washbasin in a corner of the workroom and observed great capes come to life. Some could fly, and some could make themselves and their wearers invisible. Others could make a person as large as a house, or as tiny as a mouse. There were capes that could control the weather, and a few that could go time-traveling. But the ones I most admired were the Thinking Capes. They were wise and clever. Thinking all day seemed to make them content. I longed to be one of them.

"You can think," Finch said. He couldn't keep the scorn out of his voice. "You made up all those stories."

By listening to spells that were meant for the others, I learned whatever I could. But it was stolen knowledge. Not one of the weavers suspected I was absorbing anything but the water from his hands. Then the day came when the cape makers' magic field would no longer grow a single cotton plant. No one knew why, not even the Thinking Capes. Without the special cloth, the cape makers' shop was forced to close. One of the weavers took me home, where I could still be useful, and as you see, magic cotton never wears out. Generation after generation used me as a towel until one day I was passed to the family with whom you found me.

"What about the merchant who cut off your golden strings? I guess you made that up, too?" Finch murmured. Rain had begun to fall. It dripped off the leaves and onto his hair and skin, but he didn't even notice.

I am sorry to say I invented it all. I never belonged to a merchant. I never advised anyone of anything. I never had strings until the woman who had the garage sale decided to make me into a costume for her son. After that child rejected me, I thought I was finished. I wasn't even a towel any longer. I was totally useless. Then you came along.

Fin could still recall the exact moment he'd spotted the cape on a table among old hats, umbrellas, and ladies' purses. It had looked as real as if a superhero had just taken it off. He'd never felt so desperate to have something before. "I told my mom you were the only thing I wanted for my birthday," he said.

I remember, Master. You played with me as if I were truly a magic cape. It made me think, Why not? So I dared to try and change my fate. But I knew I would have to be patient—to wait for the right time. My op-

portunity finally came when you and your friends decided to be superheroes. I felt you might accept me—and you did. The last few weeks have been the happiest time of my existence.

Finch ran a hand through his wet hair. He suddenly felt chilled. "Then why did you stop talking to me after Bud cut off your strings?" he murmured.

You gave me a chance to be something important. You believed in me. But I was not very good at thinking. I was not like the wise capes I had known. I grew afraid my advice would put you in danger. That is why I thought it would be best if I disappeared. I have been trying to remember the spell that would put me to sleep forever.

"You shouldn't have given up like that!" Finch exclaimed over the noisy patter of rain on leaves. "It isn't right! You should've kept trying." But instead of anger, he felt something else inside. It was as if a soft green thread connecting his heart to the cape were being tugged.

Finch rubbed an arm across his face. When he looked up, he was smiling a little. "I didn't think your advice was so bad. I'm not really a superhero, either."

On the contrary, Master, look what you have accom-

plished. Your sister is happier now. Your teacher is making a lot of new friends. You saved the hermit crabs.

"But I didn't have to be a superhero to do those things," Fin objected.

Perchance not. But you also saved me. That required more than courage and determination—it needed an extraordinary heart.

As if it agreed, Fin's heart beat a little quicker. "But I'm still a beginner. We all are," he said firmly. He gazed at the sky. The rain shower was passing already. "Look, the guys and I are learning how to be superheroes. And you're like a thinking-cape-in-training. But together we're a great team. That's the real secret to the Society of Secret Superheroes."

Indeed it is.

"Then you'll keep thinking?"

Gladly.

With the end of the cape, Finch dabbed the rain from the plastic covering on *Tales from the Arabian Nights*. He was looking forward to finishing "The Second Voyage of Sinbad the Sailor" later. For now, though, there was something he needed to do right away.

"Come on," he said as he wrapped his arms around the tree trunk. "We've got to climb down and call the guys. It's time to start thinking about our next mission."

Yes, Master Finch!